X'd in the Xeriscape

Lovely Lethal Gardens 24

Dale Mayer

X'D IN THE XERISCAPE: LOVELY LETHAL GARDENS, BOOK 24
Beverly Dale Mayer
Valley Publishing Ltd.

Copyright © 2024 Beverly Dale Mayer

All rights reserved. Except for use in any review, the reproduction or utilization of this work in whole or in part by any electronic, mechanical or other means, now known or hereafter invented, including xerography, photocopying and recording, or in any information storage or retrieval system, is forbidden without the written permission of the publisher.

This is a work of fiction. Names, characters, places, brands, media, and incidents are either the product of the author's imagination or are used fictitiously. Any resemblance to actual events, locales, or persons, living or dead, is entirely coincidental.

ISBN-13: 978-1-773369-90-7
Print Edition

About This Book

Riches to rags. ... Some people make plans. ... Some people change them, ... and it's chaos in the end!

Doreen loves gardens, all kinds of them. In the Okanagan, situated at the tip of the desert, water-frugal gardening makes sense. When Doreen sees a lovely xeriscaped garden from a drone video, she's fascinated. When Mack mentions a mystery surrounding the property, she is mesmerized.

Getting the details, however, is no easy feat. That's because there aren't many. But digging in and asking questions is something Doreen and her clan are good at, and it doesn't take long to delve into the mystery in a big way, ... much to Corporal Mack Moreau's disgust.

Making a nuisance of herself might work sometimes, but too often it backfires. This time is no exception, ... and no way, once Doreen is on this case, can she ever let go ...

Sign up to be notified of all Dale's releases here!
https://geni.us/DaleNews

Chapter 1

Mid-October, Sunday…

DOREEN WAS WATCHING a video on the internet the next day, with Mack stretched out on the patio beside her. "Do you guys have drones at work?" she asked.

He looked over at her. "We don't own any at the police department."

She nodded. "I always thought they would be kinda cool."

"They're more of a headache for us. You know that people take pictures they're not supposed to with that stuff."

"Oh, I never thought about that." Doreen looked up at the sky. "That would be awfully irritating."

"Yeah. I keep expecting somebody to start taking pictures of you, now that you're so famous."

"Oh, that would be terrible," she murmured, with an eye roll. "Somebody local has bought one, and he's put his videos up on the internet. I don't even know how I got this video," she noted, "but it was recommended to me, and it's going over some local properties, and the view is really cool."

"In what way?" he asked, as he sat up and faced her.

"Look at this area."

"Oh, that's Southeast Kelowna," he noted. "I remember that area. It's really beautiful up there."

"Do they have water problems?"

"Yeah, too much water."

She stared at him. "Seriously? Because this garden is xeriscaped."

He frowned at her and asked, "What the heck does that mean?"

"It's low-water gardening, so everything is done with desert plants, and you don't really need to water it at all. There's no grass. There's no greenery. It's just desert gardening."

"Interesting," he muttered. "Still, people don't necessarily want to water a garden. Plus lots of people out there have orchards and other kinds of water necessities. However, we do have droughts too."

She nodded and then pointed. "Look at this snapshot." The drone captured a really wide view of the garden. "It's beautiful."

"Of course that whole look is very specific," Mack noted. "I can't say it's my taste."

"Maybe not," she agreed.

He frowned, as he studied it. "Let me see that." He leaned in closer. "I know that property. I was up there a couple years back. The owner of the property just up and disappeared."

"What do you mean, *up and disappeared?*" she asked.

"He went to pick up equipment but never showed up there or elsewhere again. His vehicle was found down the road nearby, but no sign of him was ever discovered. No bank accounts were touched. No credit cards used. He was just gone."

"You think he booked it, maybe getting away from the wife and kids?"

Mack shrugged. "He's a missing person, but still, it's possible."

She eyed him, raised one eyebrow, and gave him a fat smile.

He shook his head. "No, don't say it."

"Why not?" she protested. "Just think. I've got the perfect title for it."

"No, no, and no," Mack declared. "What title could you even come up with for that scenario?"

She proudly said, "X'd, … as in *X'd in the Xeriscape*."

He closed his eyes slowly and moaned. "Okay, now that's a groaner."

"Yep, but it works, doesn't it? So that's next." She patted his hand and added, "Just think. It's a cold case, so I won't have to interfere in your life or your work at all."

He shook his head. "And it would be just my luck that it will turn out to be the exact opposite, and you'll trample all over one of my cases again."

"Nope, you don't have anything to do with this one. You already were there to investigate. You did your thing. It's a cold case. Now it's my turn. *X'd in the Xeriscape's* mine."

He groaned, and she burst out laughing.

Chapter 2

DOREEN STARED DOWN at the email in shock and absolute delight. After all this time the news she'd been waiting for was finally here. So she flicked through her emails, before settling back to read this one from the beginning.

Dear Doreen,

After much work and many contacts, I have both good news and bad news.

She winced at that but kept on reading, now out loud. "We've managed to sell or have offers on 90 percent of the items that we have from the house, including all the paintings and most of the lower-valued knickknack items. See a full listing attached. I don't want to go ahead with some of these because they are less money than I had hoped to get for you. However, the offers, considering the market, do seem fair. So it depends on whether you want to hang on to the still outstanding pieces and try again at a better time or if you want to sell now and clear the slate. Most of the items have sold for excellent prices and are just awaiting your confirmation. So please go over the list carefully and see what you would like to do. Personally I think the result has been outstanding, and I'm hoping that you'll be happy with the final figure attached. As soon as you have an idea what you want to do with the other items, please let me know."

At that, she opened up the attachment and took a look. She wasn't exactly sure what was disappointing because her gaze went to the bottom line. The figure there made her eyes widen, followed by deductions of expenses and commissions, with the final payout of items, currently with buyers, was well over four hundred thousand bucks. The bulk of that being from the paintings. She sat back and stared at it.

"Good Lord," she whispered fervently. *Was that even possible?*

She stared around at her almost empty house, remembering how many of the final pieces had been moved out in bulk months earlier. Nobody had any idea what some of the paintings were worth. Then this specialist had stepped in, and she had known exactly what to do with them. Doreen went back to the sheet attached and realized that all the items that were not sold were all smaller pieces and potentially not worth much money anyway. The bigger items were slated for the November auction still … And that could be many millions …

A part of her just wanted everything sold, so that it was done and finalized. She wanted to let go of them and to get as much as she could. At the same time, she also realized that Nan had put a lot of time and effort into making this inheritance as valuable as she possibly could, so Doreen didn't want to diminish her grandmother's efforts.

She pondered what to do, when the phone rang, startling her. She looked down, recognizing the number as Scott, her antiques dealer. "Hello, Scott. What's up?"

Scott laughed. "Hey, Doreen. I sent the email and then realized it is probably a whole lot easier to explain this over the phone. I have Paula, your art consultant, with me."

"I have the email open in front of me," Doreen replied excitedly. "I have to admit that I'm absolutely thrilled with the dollar figures."

"Oh, that's good," Paula stated in relief. "We never really know what the expectations are with our clients, and it all happened so fast that I wasn't sure if you were feeling any regrets, or that you've been railroaded with any of this."

"No, not at all," Doreen declared. "Not really my cup of tea. Plus, back then, I was rather desperate to have enough money to put food on the table. I guess with this, … things have improved slightly," she teased, with a chuckle. "I don't have any use for any of these items, and they're not in my style, and they aren't something that I would necessarily enjoy having around me. They're memories of my grandmother, but she's still alive and making more memories."

"And that's a lovely thing to think about," Paula replied warmly. "So let's go over the list." That took a good twenty-five minutes, and, by the time she got down to the bottom of the list, the ones not yet sold, Paula stated, "Now I do have somebody who would take all these. Individually you might hope to get, say, ten, twelve thousand for them all. However, he's offering you seven. Generally I would agree that's a very good price, but, if that's not something you're comfortable with …"

"I'm fine with it," Doreen replied. "I'm more than fine with it. This is more than I had ever expected. I just didn't want to see all Nan's hard work go down the tube with some sort of discount pricing, not when she'd spent so much time collecting everything."

"Your grandmother has an incredibly discerning eye," Paula stated, "and, if I ever get back up there again, I would love a chance to meet her. Too often we don't get to see the fruits of somebody like that, who's still alive. Most of the time these are estate sales, where the purchaser has long gone."

"Thankfully she's not long gone, and she filled this house for me," Doreen said, her tears catching in the back of her eyes. "And I will certainly let her know how well you've done with all this. … I'm astonished at this total figure."

"I wasn't sure if you understood how the commission worked."

"I'm learning," Doreen noted in a dry tone. "Obviously, for all the work that you do, this is how you get paid."

"Exactly," Paula confirmed, "and we do belong to a very large company and are very reputable, and we are insured. Thus, we confirm that all the sales proceeds come through properly. Yet you are paying for a lot more than just commissions."

"Of course, and how does the process work from here?"

Paula chuckled. "It's pretty simple. I need the paperwork back that was attached to the email—the sooner, the better—indicating whether you want me to go ahead with these other items that we have offers for."

"Yes, I do," Doreen interrupted.

"Okay, good. In that case we should probably cut you a check within about thirty days, forty-five at the most," she shared, "depends on the billing circle and how quickly I can get all these sales locked in."

"Perfect," Doreen replied in delight. "That sounds absolutely wonderful."

"Good, I'm glad to hear that," Paula stated. "This has

been a lot of fun. We don't often get such an eclectic mix of items, so it's been taxing to find the right people, but it's also been a good challenge. So I really appreciate you letting me come in and help you out with this."

After a few more moments of going over the details, Doreen ended the call and stared down at the email again. She couldn't wait to share this good news with Mack and Nan. Right now, she was stunned, and she herself had to process this awesome news. It was almost impossible to believe the amount of money coming to her, money that, when she was married and living with Mathew, wouldn't have meant anything because she didn't handle the money. She was given a certain amount to cover her personal needs, and everything else was handled by Mathew. But now, this money would be hers and hers alone.

Not only that, but it was also a huge gift that had come from Nan, who had obviously planned for it many years ago. Doreen couldn't even contemplate setting up something like this, if she had children or grandchildren of her own. To think Nan had that kind of foresight was just amazing. It was also humbling to realize how lucky Doreen was to have Nan as part of her family and to know that she had always been so concerned about the future that she had set up such a thing.

Even if it was just a fluke that she'd set it up, it was still one of those awe-inspiring deals, and Nan had wanted Doreen to do something in her own way. Sure, she was helping a lot of people with the cold cases she was solving, but she also should lock up some of this money, so she wouldn't be broke ever again. That meant finding somebody who would be there to give her a hand in making sound investments.

She wasn't even sure who that advisor would be. Sure,

she had Mack and Nan and Nick and a few people to talk to and to help her find somebody and to ensure the advisor was honest. Of course honesty at this point in time was a whole different story.

She opened the kitchen door and stepped outside and stared up at what had now become an absolutely glorious day.

Too excited to contain herself, on the spur of the moment, she raced outside and did cartwheels down the lawn, with Mugs and Thaddeus racing behind her. Mugs barked and barked and barked, as she came to a crazy hair-flinging, face-flushing stop, close to the river, and collapsed on the grass, laughing. He climbed all over her, with Thaddeus not to be outdone, as he was squawking and seemingly trying to imitate her cartwheels.

"Oh my goodness, Thaddeus." Doreen laughed, her face flushed with joy. "I'm not sure what you're trying to do, but wow."

He flew up into the air and landed just before her and hopped even closer, before finally landing on her belly. Mugs slid off to the side ever-so-slightly, reached out a paw, and almost knocked Thaddeus off. Thaddeus turned on him, squawked and pecked at him with his beak. Chaos took over for a moment, until things calmed down, and she sat here, just happy to have the bickering done with, her animals now lying in peace at her side, well, almost. Thaddeus had taken up residence on her shoulder again and was humming gently in her ear, making her cuddle him closer. She remained here for a bit and smiled at the world around her.

"It's a great time to be alive," she murmured. She stretched out her arms and legs, then nestled her arms behind her head and just stared up at the sky. Such a sense of well-being and joy filled her that she couldn't believe it. The money was enough to stop her worries about her future, and it would also stave off starvation for a very long time. Just the $7,000 for selling the knickknacks to a proposed buyer would keep her in food forever, it seemed, and that just made her heart swell. She couldn't wait to tell Mack. However, she felt conflicted about calling him at work to interrupt his day. He would probably be by later today or tonight, and she would tell him then for sure.

As she remained here on the grass, with a huge smile on her face, she basked in the glory of the sales, until her phone rang. "Hi, Nan!"

"Are you all right, dear?" Nan asked. She had obviously sensed Doreen's excitement.

"I'm better than all right," she exclaimed.

After a moment of silence, Nan cautiously asked, "Are you sure? You sound awfully excited."

Doreen sat upright and quickly told her about the news.

"Oh, that's lovely," Nan cried out. "That sounds like decent money for all my efforts too."

"That's what I was hoping you would say," Doreen replied. "You have no idea how grateful I am that you did this for me. … It's just unbelievable that there should be such a huge payout."

"I don't know about *unbelievable*," Nan noted cautiously. "I did put in a lot of effort to ensure we got good pieces."

"I appreciate that. I really do," Doreen shared. "I was pretty stunned when Scott and Paula called me this morning. I have to do the paperwork Paula sent, regarding all the smaller items," she noted, bounding to her feet. "I came outside, screaming for joy and running around my garden and doing cartwheels. Then I completely forgot I have to print off the paperwork and send it in."

"You better do that right now," Nan stated. "Afterward, why don't you come down for tea?"

"Sure, I can do that," Doreen agreed. "That sounds lovely."

Doreen rang off and, with the animals running at her side, she rushed into the house, where she quickly printed off the paperwork, signed everything, scanned it in, and emailed it back to her curator. With that done, and the animals at her side, she headed to Nan's. Doreen didn't even know how to or what to do to show Nan appreciation for everything that she had done because this was massive. This was life-altering huge.

It hadn't really struck home before. Sure, there'd been talk about Nan's antiques, all kinds of projected numbers regarding their sale, plus the paintings and the rare books, but it really hadn't sunk in yet just how much some of these items would bring in reality. Even when she did think about the current sales in terms of dollar figures, she didn't think in terms of *those kind* of numbers because it was just … wow. This was beyond life-changing. This was completely unbelievable, and she couldn't be happier. She was still bouncing and singing to herself, as she made it down to Nan's.

Chapter 3

NAN TOOK ONE look at her granddaughter's face and chuckled. She opened her arms, and Doreen gave her the gentlest of hugs. Mugs, not to be outdone, jumped up against Nan's knees looking for cuddles. Nan, trying to pet Mugs and hold Thaddeus, who was trying to walk onto her shoulder from Doreen's, laughed in sheer joy.

"You have no idea what a gift you've given me," Doreen murmured, suddenly teary-eyed.

"Oh, don't you dare cry," Nan scolded as she reached up to help Thaddeus stabilize on her narrow shoulder. "That'll make me cry." And, within minutes, the two women were both wiping away the tears from their eyes. Nan chuckled. "I am so happy to hear that all of my fun—and remember it was fun, spending all those years finding just the right furnishings—produced something worthwhile. You never really know if you can trust a lot of people out there, but it seems we did pretty well after all."

"We?" Doreen repeated, as she shook her head. "*You* did phenomenal. I didn't do anything."

"Oh, you're the one who went through the process and managed to get this much sold," Nan pointed out. "You don't realize how big that is. Sit down. Sit down," Nan said waving at the table where Mugs had taken up residence, an expectant look on his face. Goliath had claimed the closest planter box to take a long nap and ignored everyone.

"Let's get the tea." And, with that, she bustled into the kitchen.

Doreen sat outside on the patio, her heart still so full and tears still in the corner of her eyes, filled with gratitude for everything that her grandmother had done. Such an amazing gift. And she felt so sorry for everybody else in the world who hadn't had the same benefit of someone like her grandmother.

When Nan came bustling out again, carrying a full pot of tea, Doreen bounded to her feet and offered, "Here. Let me take it."

Nan just ignored her and put the pot of tea on her patio table. "It's fine," Nan said. "I'm a long way away from being an invalid."

"Invalid. Invalid," Thaddeus squawked loudly.

"Ha! Besides, even if you become an invalid," Doreen noted, chuckling, "you'll be a feisty one."

"You're darn right," Nan declared, beaming. "Life's too short for anything other than that." And, with that, she frowned at Doreen, "Now, I don't have any treats for you today. I'm sorry about that."

"I will survive," Doreen stated, yet disappointed. She just didn't want Nan to see it. And then Nan heard something, and she tilted her head to the side and asked, "Was that my door?"

"I don't know." Doreen frowned at her. "I didn't hear anything."

Just then Richie called out, "Hey, Nan, is that you?"

"Who else do you expect it to be?" she replied in exasperation, still seated. "You knocked on my door."

Richie walked through Nan's apartment onto her patio, took one look, and beamed at Doreen. "Now isn't that perfect timing?" And he held out a little basket.

Nan bounded to her feet, raced over, took one look, and chortled.

That's exactly how Doreen could describe it. Nan literally was chortling. She and Thaddeus were two of a kind. And right now both heads were peering into the basket like it was Christmas. "It must be good stuff," Doreen noted, looking at her grandmother in amusement. "I haven't heard a sound out of you like that before."

Nan glared at her and then beamed. "It's cookies. Fresh warm cookies." She whipped off the cloth on top, so even Doreen could get a whiff of the chocolate.

"Oh my," she muttered, as she looked at Richie. "Were you just in the kitchen, raiding these straight from the oven?"

"I always raid the kitchen," he declared and then shrugged. "They're used to me by now."

Doreen laughed. "I'm sure everybody in this place is used to you by now," she said, with a smile.

He nodded with a fat grin and gave her a side look. "So it should be. We pay plenty to be here."

Doreen didn't say anything in response but smiled, knowing that, if Nan ever ran out of money for this place, Doreen would be capable of at least keeping Nan in the style she was used to. At least Doreen hoped so. She wasn't sure how much Nan spent on all her cronies here, but it was important that Doreen had a way to give back, if needed.

Richie pointed at the empty chair. "Since I brought the

goodies, do I get to sit with you?"

"Absolutely," Nan said, as she shuffled her chair over so that there was room.

He nudged the basket toward Doreen. "You better grab one. This is your nan's favorite cookie."

Doreen smiled and suggested, "Maybe she should get one first then."

"Nope, not at all," Nan argued, "but hurry up, child. I can't wait. Warm cookies only stay warm for a certain amount of time."

Still laughing, Doreen reached inside the basket and grabbed a cookie and took a bite. "Oh my." Warm melted chocolate filled her mouth. She closed her eyes in delight. "You guys have some of the best cooks here."

"Right," Richie agreed. "We're so happy you got rid of that other one."

Doreen rolled her eyes at him. "I would hardly say I got rid of her."

"Sure, you did," he repeated, grinning.

"And believe me. We're grateful." Nan was almost giddy, as she waved around her cookie.

Doreen burst out laughing. "Happy to help," she conceded.

"What's your newest case?" Richie asked.

She pondered that. "It's not that I have a new case," she clarified, "but I do have a curiosity."

At that, the other two stopped and looked at her. "We like curiosities," Nan declared, leaning forward eagerly.

"What kind of a curiosity?" Richie prodded.

"I saw some drone footage of a house up in the Southeast Kelowna area, and the yard had been xeriscaped."

Nan nodded; Richie looked completely blank. "Xeri

what?" he asked in confusion.

"Xeriscaped. It was converted to a low-water garden, like a walking garden, a desert-variety garden."

"Oh, like my backyard when I don't water it," he quipped, with a smirk.

Doreen stared at him and then slowly nodded. "Yeah, I guess that would be one form of xeriscape." Then she shook her head. "In this case, lots of rocks and desert plants."

He nodded. "But, up in that area, there is a lot of water. Lots of big properties, huge estates up there. That's quite an expansive area."

"This property has a smaller front yard," she explained, "and it could have a lot of space in the backyard, but I didn't see it."

"Go on. Go on," Nan said, telling Richie to *shush*.

Thaddeus immediately picked up his cue. "Sssshush. Sssshush."

Everyone laughed but looked at Doreen expectantly.

"Anyway, the whole front yard had been divided into walkways and quadrants, and the way that the drone caught the image from overhead, I saw an *X* in the front yard, and the design put different kinds of rocks in each triangle inside the *X*."

"What's that got to do with anything?" Richie asked, staring at Doreen. Then he turned to glare at Nan. "Don't you *shush* me again. She's taking her sweet time."

"I know. I know, but we have to give her some time to get it out too," Nan whispered in a low voice. "She does not always explain herself very clearly."

"*Anyway*, Mack knew the property because the owner had upped and disappeared from one day to the next, … a couple years back."

They stopped and stared at her. "And?" Richie asked. "What's that got to do with anything?"

"Well, it is a curiosity," she repeated, staring at him, "because how many people do you know just up and disappear and never show up again?"

"*Never?*" he repeated, his eyebrows shooting up. "What about credit cards? What about bank statements? Did he take his truck?"

"His vehicle was found a few blocks away, parked but empty. He was supposedly on his way to pick up equipment, and yet the truck was found abandoned near his home. He didn't arrive at work. The vehicle was found later that day just a few blocks away—once his wife started calling around to see where he was."

"Did she check the bars?" Richie teased, with a chuckle.

"I don't know. I haven't spoken to her. Mack told me that this guy is still a missing person and that the case has been open for a while now. Although I have to find out exactly how many years ago he disappeared." She pondered that, then pulled out her phone and texted Mack, with a smirk. **Regarding our *X* case, what was the name of the missing man? And when did he disappear?** She sent the message. "I don't know how long it will take Mack to get back to me. … I didn't get all the details, which is bad for me," she admitted. "This morning I expected to speak with him about those, but I haven't had a chance as of yet."

"Right," Richie agreed. "I'm not sure I ever heard anything about it." He turned and looked at Nan. "What about you?"

Nan sat here, sipping her tea, with a far-off look in her eyes. "You know," she shook her head and added, "I feel like something is there, but I can't quite pull it out of my brain."

She gave her head a shake. "Even shaking my head is not helping," she said in disgust.

Doreen stared at her. "Please tell me that you don't think that shaking your head will work, right?"

"Hey, it works like magic," Richie declared.

"What does?" Doreen asked, still staring at her grandmother.

"When she shakes her head harder, things that she's forgotten pop back in again," Richie explained, as if that were normal.

Doreen slowly rubbed her temples. "Okay, I can't say I've ever heard of that being effective."

"Well, here at Rosemoor," Nan declared, "we've got all kinds of tricks to remember things. We do have memory problems, dear, so we are a little bit more forward-thinking in terms of our solutions. And still, lots of people don't want to listen to us, saying that *we forget things*, as if it's almost a given." She rolled her eyes. "It's *not* a given, and none of us want to listen to that kind of garbage anyway." Nan *harrumphed*.

Doreen nodded and kept her mouth shut on that topic because that was a conversation she could not win anyway. "I just wondered if maybe either of you had heard anything about the case. I'm not much help if I don't have the name of the people involved."

"I presume somebody was left behind," Nan noted. "You mentioned the wife phoned around?"

At that, Doreen nodded. "Yes, but I don't have any details about who she is, or even what date we are talking about."

"Oh, in that case," Richie stated, "you really do need to get all your facts before you come to us for help. You know that, right?"

She completely ignored the fact that he was the one who wanted the details and that she wasn't trying to get their assistance just yet, but that was another argument she could not win. She just smiled at him. "I'll get the details. Don't you worry."

"Of that I'm sure. Likely Mack is already pulling up all that information for you." Richie chuckled.

The next forty minutes was fun but also frustrating, as neither of the two people at the table with Doreen could remember anything about the case. Then, all of a sudden, Nan stared at Doreen and said, "Dennis Polanski."

Doreen froze and asked, "Dennis who?"

"Dennis Polanski," Richie cried out.

She frowned at him. "Okay, so apparently you two know that name."

"Sure, I know that name." He looked over at Nan and then nodded. "Good one."

"Well, that's nice," Doreen noted, "but what's a good one?"

"I shook my head enough that it came loose," Nan declared proudly.

"Okay, good." Doreen frowned. "What does that name mean to you?"

Nan looked at her, surprised. "That's the person who went missing." She stared at her granddaughter.

"Dennis Polanski is the man who went missing?"

"That's what I just said." Nan shook her head and made an odd noise. "Maybe you should shake your head every once in a while."

Doreen grinned at her. "I often do, when it comes to your and Richie's antics," she shared, with a smile.

Nan snorted. "Okay, maybe so, but that's the man who got up one day and never came home again. And we heard all kinds of rumors about it, didn't we?" She looked over at Richie.

"Yes, but I don't remember the details," he admitted. "That was a long time ago."

"It was only maybe eight, nine years ago?" Nan added. She looked at Doreen for confirmation.

"I have no idea about that. Mack thought it was just a couple years back," she replied. "That's why I need the file, so I can get the dates locked down, before we can go forward with this case."

"The dates will be important." Richie nodded. "When you think about it, we could be looking all over the place for this person. He might have chosen to up and disappear, you know?"

"Tell me what you remember about it," Doreen said.

Nan shrugged and grimaced. "Nothing. I just know what the news shared, which is that he went missing. Left for work one day, didn't show up, and that's it. Nobody heard from him again."

"Amazing," Doreen muttered. "I just never quite understood how somebody could disappear like that."

"Well, obviously he didn't disappear on his own," Nan declared, staring at her granddaughter. "That's pretty obvious."

Just then Goliath shifted, jumping into Doreen's lap and filling it as he curled up to go back to sleep. She wrapped her arms around him and pulled him closer.

"Yet, if he wanted to leave an unhappy marriage, or maybe he'd stolen something at work or just got up one day and decided he wouldn't live like that anymore, that's exactly what they do." Doreen gazed at her grandmother as Goliath stretched out a paw and tapped her on the cheek. "They decide they're done, and they get up and leave."

Nan frowned at her and then at Richie and shrugged. "But that's being a quitter. Can't say I know very many people like that. ... No, that's not true," Nan clarified. "I know a lot of people like that. It's just not the kind of people I choose to hang out with."

"Understood." Doreen agreed because, if there was one thing her grandmother wasn't, it was a quitter.

Nan suggested, "We also have to understand that maybe something bad happened to him, and it wasn't that he was quitting life at all. It was more a case of somebody got life to quit on him."

Richie chuckled at that. "Good play on words, but I'm sure you'll get to the bottom of it, Doreen." He rubbed his hands together. "This is exciting, and here I had no idea, when we got up this morning, that there would be something new and different going on."

Nan beamed. "You can always count on Doreen to come up with something exciting and new."

"I don't know about that," Doreen replied cautiously. "An awful lot goes on in this world that I don't have anything to do with."

"Oh, but there's a lot less now," Nan declared. "You are heavily involved in so much, and I'm so proud of you."

"What? For being a busybody? Sticking my nose in everything?" she teased in a wry tone. A second paw patted her cheek, making Doreen chuckle as she half leaned over, half lifted Goliath and kissed him on the top of his head.

Nan chuckled. "Busybody with a purpose. That's what detectives are too, you know? And I know you're not licensed. I know you're not in law enforcement." Nan gave a wave of her hand, as if none of that was important. "Yet you're doing what you can do." Nan eyed Doreen intently. "That's more than a lot of people do."

Richie nodded. "And that's a fact. Lots of people don't do very much because they don't want to get involved," he explained, "but you've never been afraid of that. You just jump right in."

"Even if I shouldn't," she quipped, with a chuckle.

He beamed at her. "Yeah, even then," he confirmed, not pulling his punches. "We really admire that. We admire that adventurous spirit you have and that you go where nobody else would dare to go. It makes us happy, makes us realize just how good you are at living."

"Versus?" she asked, not sure where he was going with that.

"Versus *existing*," he pointed out. "So many people just exist. They don't really understand that there's more to life than just sitting there and doing nothing."

She nodded at that. "I guess that makes sense too," she conceded, "but a lot of people would do more if they could do more."

"You made sure that you could do more," Nan stated, "and, for that, we're all grateful. You keep us on our toes. Now look at this case, if you hadn't asked for that information, I wouldn't have kept rattling my brain around until it came free." She chuckled at the end.

"Wow. Still I would appreciate it if you don't rattle your brain so much that you hurt yourself," Doreen added.

Nan went off in a peal of laughter. "Not going to happen. I've got way too much going on in my life for that to happen."

And that was the truth, as far as Doreen could see. So much was going on in her grandmother's head that Doreen couldn't imagine anything wrong happening. Still, too many things had happened wrong in Doreen's life that she didn't want to take a chance. "I get that. Just make sure you keep it in control. I'll go do some research to see if I can find this person. *Polanski. Dennis Polanski.* Maybe I'll stop at the library afterward."

"Do you really get much information from the library?" Nan asked curiously.

"Sometimes, yes. Depends how old this information is. I start with Google searches, and then I follow up those leads until I run out of more leads, and then I have to find another source for information," she explained. "Sometimes I hassle poor Mack, and sometimes I have to go to the source and hit the library again and again. … The archives are pretty interesting, especially if we're looking for old information on the same person. And of course there are the Solomon files …"

The other two just nodded, as if they had a clue what she was talking about, but Doreen suspected they didn't.

"Anyway," she said, as she slowly got to her feet, "I'll head back now and try to sort it out."

"Good," Nan declared. "Keep us apprised of your progress, and we'll do a little asking around here and see if anybody knew what happened or has the scoop on it." She winked at Doreen. "You never know what we could find out here."

"Knowing this place," Doreen admitted, with a chuckle, "you probably will have it solved before next Sunday."

"Oh my, I would hope so." And, with that, Nan waved a hand at Doreen and said, "Go on, dear. Go on. You need to get started."

With a headshake, Doreen gathered her animals, gave her grandmother a kiss, and whispered, "You look after yourself."

Chapter 4

As Doreen headed toward the river, she heard Richie and Nan, their heads together, buzzing behind her, probably setting up a plan of attack on how to get more information out of Rosemoor residents and their relatives, and that was good because they were a huge valuable source of viable information for Doreen. It was just frustrating that sometimes they seemed to have better access to local sources than Doreen did.

But then she didn't have a group of cronies who had been around since forever. She only had the basic means to find stuff, like the internet, the library, and even the local phone book. She was still smiling at those ideas, when she made her way home again.

As she passed Richard's fence, she heard somebody singing softly. She stopped to listen, and, when she wouldn't keep moving, Mugs barked at her. "*Shh*, quiet, Mugs."

At that, the singing stopped.

She sighed. "Don't know who's singing, but it's beautiful. You certainly don't need to stop on my account." There was a loud *harrumph*, and she recognized Richard's tone.

"Eavesdropping now?" He snorted.

"Nope, not eavesdropping," she corrected, calling over the fence, "just walking home from a visit with Nan."

"Yeah, Rosemoor, that den of iniquity," he replied. "The people down there are crazy."

"I don't know about crazy." Doreen frowned. "The ones I deal with are very good-hearted."

"*Sure* they are," he quipped. "They are also nosy, interfering busybodies."

She winced because, well, there was really no way to argue with that. "Maybe," she admitted, "but only for a good cause."

"Yeah, how many more good causes could you possibly get involved in?" he muttered.

"Sorry about your brother. I'm sure that must have been pretty tough." There was silence in response to that, and then she added, "By the way, do you know a Dennis Polanski?"

"You mean, *did* I know a Dennis Polanski? He disappeared—what, a decade ago?"

"Something like that." She wandered slowly toward her kitchen door and just then Richard's head popped over the top of the fence.

He glared at her. "So now you'll interfere in somebody else's life?"

She studied him, seeing the same distress as he'd had over the previous case, involving his brother. "As I told you, I'm sorry for your brother and how that all worked out."

He nodded slowly and gave her a grudging nod. "At least … he has answers now."

"Exactly," she agreed. "They're just generally not the answers we want."

"Well, nobody would ever have thought that his friend

would have done this," Richard stated grudgingly. "It's made him very sad."

"And, for that, he'll need you," she suggested. "Sometimes good things happen to people, but other times it's not so good, and they need the support of people around them."

He glared at her. "He would have been just fine, if you hadn't gone and blown apart his world."

"Would he have, though?" she asked, staring at him. "As you just pointed out, this way he has answers."

And, with that, he shot her one more fulminating look and then disappeared over his side of the fence.

As she neared her kitchen door, she added, "You sure have a lovely voice."

"It wasn't me," he groaned.

She smiled because she was pretty sure it was him, yet she still had no idea who else was on the other side of that darn fence. One of these days, she would like to find out, but that would take a little bit more effort than she was prepared to do right now. Richard had been very voluble about his privacy, and she'd yet to be invited over.

But then it wasn't her job to worry about him. He seemed to be doing just fine, and, as long as she stayed on her side of the fence, chances were they could remain friends—if that's what they were.

She wasn't even sure about that because she'd brought an awful lot of things down on his head, more than he needed or was comfortable with. Still, she hadn't tried to hurt anybody, and hopefully people would understand that better, as time went on. But she wasn't so sure with Richard. Seemed like everybody had a different idea as to Doreen's motives.

As she walked inside her kitchen, she propped open the

kitchen door, so the animals could come and go, and brought her laptop outside. If the light would allow her, she could work out here. If not, she would have to go back inside and sit at the kitchen table. Outside, the animals milled around for a little bit and then threw themselves down into a contented slump on the carpet of grass all around her.

She smiled. "We owe Mack and the other guys so much. This is a lovely thing they did for me," she murmured, looking at her backyard, a place of beauty, where she absolutely adored being. A place where she could be herself and relax. It was such a lovely reminder of the good things about humanity.

Chapter 5

DOREEN GOT UP and stretched, rotated her neck, and sat back down again. She was almost done going through everything that she could find online about Dennis Polanski, and, so far, there wasn't a whole lot. Even the news reports were scarce on the details, and there'd been several articles entitled, "Have You Seen this Man?"

Lots of people asked for information. A reward was posted. Doreen pondered that, as she made herself a sandwich and then grimaced at it and sighed. "Even after all this time, you still default to a sandwich. You should be cooking more," she muttered. Of course, as the weather cooled ahead, she would have to do more cooking because sandwiches just wouldn't cut it. Still, this was easy when she was working. She almost laughed at that because people all over the world said things like that. Whatever was fast and easy, they were good with. Doreen craved some almond chicken gai ding from the local Chinese restaurant, but eating out wasn't in the budget.

At that thought, she froze because her financial condition was changing pretty fast, and maybe she could go get something from her favorite restaurant here. *Maybe I can.*

Maybe I should. As a celebration?

Still, she needed to focus on this missing person, and, if she solved something or got somewhere, then maybe she could look at that as a reward. Yet food as a reward was probably the worst thing she could do. Still, she was getting pretty tired of all the *shoulds* and *shouldn'ts* in her world, even now, some six months or so of living alone. However, it was probably hard for just half a year to wipe out all the regulations she had lived under with Mathew for the fourteen years of their marriage. She kind of went crazy initially with her newfound freedom. Yet, without money, she couldn't have gone too crazy, and now she would have to watch her spending even more closely because she *would* have money, yet she must be frugal with it. This money must last her for a lifetime.

She just smiled, continued on with her research, poring over articles. When the phone rang a little bit later, she glanced at her screen. "Hey, Mack," she greeted him. "How are you doing?"

"I'm doing fine. … How are you? You've been suspiciously quiet."

"*Really?*" she asked in a mocking tone. "I leave you alone, so you can get some work done, and here you're suspicious about what I might be doing in the meantime?"

"Yeah," he admitted. "I mean, it is you."

She chuckled. "It is, indeed, me," she murmured. "I'm researching that missing person's case."

"Oh, right. I forgot about that."

"Well, I haven't," she replied. "Dennis Polanski, wasn't it?"

"Yes, exactly. I doubt that you found out much."

"I did text you, but you didn't give me any names or

dates yet."

"Right, I was calling for another reason," he said. "What are you up to right now?"

"I'm just about to eat a sandwich." After a moment of silence, she sighed heavily. "I know. I know. *I know.* I should be eating something other than sandwiches."

He burst out laughing. "See? I didn't even need to say anything."

"No, I was sitting here, reminding myself that I needed to do more cooking. As winter approaches, I'll want warmer food because cold food won't necessarily be something I want to eat."

"Right," Mack agreed, "and making a good homemade soup isn't hard either."

She perked up at that idea. "That sounds good. ... Do you know how to make soup?"

He chuckled. "Yeah, soup's one of the easiest things in the world."

She beamed. "In that case, I would really like some soup."

"That's fine. We can pick one or two recipes, and we'll have a cooking session.'

"Oh, I would love to do that," she said. "Are you okay with any kind of soup?"

He hesitated. "I suspect the soups that you're used to are very different from the soups I'm used to," he noted cautiously. "So I'll say, yes, but maybe not."

She burst out laughing. "Is this really you saying something like that?" she asked in a teasing voice.

"Yeah, sure is. Believe me. I know that you've been used to a very different level of food."

"Doesn't matter what I was used to because it's what I

have now that matters. And, by the way," she added, her voice breaking in excitement, "I didn't get a chance to tell you about the phone call. Email *and* phone call," she corrected.

"From whom? Tell me." She quickly filled him in on Paula's email and the phone call with Scott and Paula. "How much?" he repeated in astonishment, when she read off the figure.

"I know," she cried out. "Isn't that incredible? And that's all from that little stuff and the paintings."

"Wow."

"Right? I know." She chuckled. "It's huge."

"That's one word for it," he replied cautiously. "I'm not sure that's the word I would have used, but it is pretty magnificent."

"It is, indeed," she declared. "It will still be at least a month or so before I get anything though."

"Oh, yeah. I'm sure they've got to go through all kinds of accounting systems. How did Nan take it?"

"She seemed pretty happy about it all, but I'm not sure the amount even surprised her."

"You know, given what you've done so far, I wouldn't be at all surprised if it was just completely commonplace for her," Mack pointed out. "I am thrilled for you. That's a huge amount of money."

"I certainly won't have to starve anymore."

He burst out laughing. "Considering you haven't starved yet," he said, "I don't think that's an issue."

"I haven't," she murmured, "but it always felt like I was on the edge."

"So now pull yourself back off that edge," he ordered, "and figure out what kind of soup you want."

"I will. Now do you have anything on that cold case you can give me?" she asked. "If you could nail down how long he's been missing, that would be a great help. You said a couple years, which I take to mean two or three. Yet Richie is saying eight or nine, and then my neighbor said a decade. So check your records and clarify with me."

Mack clearly hesitated. "Probably got it confused with another case, since I wasn't looking at the file on Dennis at the time."

She added, "I don't know how much of it is even in the public realm. I haven't been down to the library yet."

"I think I can give you a bunch of information," he replied, "but, just so we are on the up-and-up, let me clear it with the captain first."

"Okay." She didn't have a problem with him doing that, especially after she'd helped the captain on a personal cold case of his own. Although she tried not to push the boundaries of what info she was allowed, but, hey, she wasn't against asking for information on a cold case that was pretty well accessible by almost anybody.

By the time Mack rang off, she was already on Google, searching for soups, trying to remember the favorite kind of soups that she used to love. There was a ham and potato, one that she had been absolutely in love with but could never have because her husband had always kept that off the menu because, apparently she would gain weight with it.

And then she remembered goulash, which she wasn't sure was a soup. She pondered that and wrote down a bunch of the soups, hoping that maybe one of them would work for Mack. Just because she may want these soups didn't mean that he could make them. Although he seemed to be pretty open to trying anything, something that she really could learn from him. He'd been very good to her and for her in so many ways.

That reminded her how she had heard nothing from her ex about their pending divorce. That was getting to be a pain too. Mathew had supposedly signed paperwork at his attorney's office, and then she didn't know what happened afterward. She sent Nick a text message, asking if there'd been any progress on the Mathew front. Instead of texting her back, he phoned her. "Hey," she greeted him. "I was just having such a great day that I figured that, as long as I had good news coming from some direction, maybe I should check and see if there was any good news from you."

He burst out laughing. "I don't know what's the good news that you already got today, but it seems that you've been on quite a roll recently."

"Seems like it." She laughed. "That's a good thing."

"Of course. You've been helping all kinds of people."

"Maybe, but I think I'm also pissing off a lot of people."

"I think that goes with the territory," he noted, and she could sense the smile in his voice. "Anyway, as far as your ex, he did send the paperwork and, of course, again a signature is missing."

She glared at the phone. "So, in other words, he's still playing games."

"Not sure about that. I did talk to his lawyer, and the lawyer was vexed, but he'd missed it because he'd gone over it with Mathew ahead of time. So I've just gotten off the phone with his attorney again this morning, and he said that he has new documents, and they're coming our way today."

"But do we trust him to deliver on that?"

"No, not until we get them," Nick stated cheerfully, "but we are getting closer."

"Still seems like games. And, by the way," she added, with a little hesitation, "once he does sign, and we have an agreement in place, I know it sounds terrible to ask … but can I get a small advance?"

"*Ahhh.*"

"It's not that I'm broke, you understand."

"No, we don't want you broke either," he said, his tone severe. "We should make some of it happen pretty fast. He might be given some time to sell assets, so he can ask for a certain amount of time before he has to pay up."

"Of course he will." She groaned. "Here I was so hoping that we could get this dealt with, and then I could get some money."

"Yeah, that's what I am hoping. Regardless, we are almost there."

"And … this sounds terrible."

"What's the terrible part?" he asked curiously. "For you to say something is *terrible*, I can't imagine."

"It just occurred to me. What happens to my divorce if he dies before he signs all the papers?"

"Yeah, considering how many people you deal with who have died in the past or are dying, I won't say that that's an unusual question to ask," he explained in a pensive tone. "And, matter of fact, *most* people would ask about that, especially given how long the actual process can take. Plus, life being *life*."

"Will I still get my money?"

"It depends," he hedged. "If we could get something locked down, yes. Would you get all of it? Depends on who else is in the will and how much else has to be sorted and sold. And things then might have to be sold at a cheaper price."

"So, in other words, don't even go there."

"Not unless you're still in his will," he stated cheerfully, "in which case you get it all."

"I don't think I am," she replied. "I would have thought Robin would have been. Although now that she's gone, I don't know."

"I don't know that Robin was even in there to begin with. Mathew's relationship with her didn't last very long."

"Maybe not, but he was pretty enamored with her."

At that, Nick chuckled. "I don't think so. It seemed to me to have been more of a use-and-abuse type of relationship."

"But they were both so good at that," she murmured.

"And it's not your problem, unless you were planning on killing him."

She burst out laughing. "Nope, sure wasn't, but I have to admit to a moment of worry, if he did die ahead of time, that I wouldn't get anything. After all, look at the people he hung out with."

"You will still get something. I can't guarantee it'll be the same amount, but you should get at least close to that. If not more so because, if he died and didn't leave a will, you would be the next person in line to inherit because you're legally his wife."

"Even though we're estranged?"

"Yes, because, as long as he hasn't fully signed the divorce settlement document, you're still legally his partner."

"Wow. He would hate that," she murmured.

"Maybe, but I would be perfectly okay with it." At that, he rang off.

Chapter 6

Monday Morning...

THE NEXT MORNING Doreen woke to the ringing of her phone. She reached over and answered it, still groggy.

"Did you find anything?" Nan asked in a rapid tone.

"Find what?" Doreen asked, rubbing the sleep out of her eyes. "What time is it?"

Nan asked, "Are you still in bed?"

"Yes," she replied in exasperation. "I still don't even know what time it is."

"It's almost seven."

"Seven?" she repeated. "Since when do you call me this early?"

"I'm heading out to practice lawn bowling, and I wanted to touch base with you beforehand."

"Okay," she muttered, still rubbing her face. "I haven't found anything, if that's what you are calling about."

"Oh, dear, that's not very good. I'll talk to you later." And, with that, Nan disconnected.

Doreen flopped back onto the bed. "*Great*, nothing like making me feel bad."

And, of course, that's not why Nan had called. However,

it would just add to that sense of Doreen *should* be doing better. Not that there was a whole lot better to do, but hey. She got up, grabbed a shower, and, as she was getting dressed, Mack phoned.

"The captain okayed you to have the information," he shared, "but again it'll be kept private."

"I got that," she said, as she yawned.

"Are you okay?"

"Yeah, Nan woke me up, asking if I'd found anything out on this case."

"Already?" he asked in amazement.

"Yes, she was heading off to lawn bowling or something," she explained in disgust. "You know it's not worth talking to me until I get coffee."

"I do know that," he stated, amused. "I did hesitate to call you at this hour."

"Ha, ha, ha," she quipped. "I'm here. I'm fine, and I am dealing with the lack of coffee issue."

"Good." He chuckled. "In that case it should be okay to keep talking to you."

"Of course it is," she muttered. "Besides there has to be some information out there in order to find this person."

"Oh, you'll probably find him," he noted in a sardonic tone, "just to make us all look like idiots."

"Oh, ouch. By the way, I contacted your brother, asked how Mathew and the signatures were going, and Mathew's attorney apparently sent something, but it was missing one dratted signature again."

"So he is back to his antics, *huh*? I'm heading into a meeting. I'll email you the stuff afterward."

She ended the call, headed downstairs with all her animals, and put on the coffee. At least Mack understood her need for coffee. Nan apparently didn't understand time frames. But then Nan was getting up earlier and earlier every day. Doreen had heard that was common with older people but hadn't really seen it, except now Nan was definitely heading in that direction. It was kind of irritating and also sweet that she would call. But the irritation was winning out, at least until Doreen had coffee.

While the coffee brewed, Doreen fed all her animals, her trio scarfing down the food like she had never fed them before. Shaking her head at how hungry they appeared to be, she pointed out, "Hey, I feed all you guys morning and night, with treats in-between, and none of you look starved either. I guess you like your groceries too, *huh*?" She had to laugh at that. "Don't you guys worry. You will never run out of food now for sure."

As soon as she had a cup of coffee in her hand, she opened up the kitchen door, and the animals now raced outside with her. She went to the patio, sat down with a heavy *clunk* and surveyed the yard and the morning ahead of her. She really needed to remember to be grateful for everything that she had. Yet, without the coffee, it was really hard to do anything except be a grump. That almost made her smile. She blew some of the hot steam away on the coffee and finally managed her first sip. She sat with a smile on her face, as the caffeine slowly worked through her system.

"Now that was a reason to get out of bed," she murmured to herself. She took several more sips and then put down the cup to enjoy it slowly. She watched a squirrel scamper across the lawn, another one chasing behind it. The antics of all these animals made her heart smile. She had everything here, from field mice to rabbits and the occasional deer that wandered down to access the river.

Because her property was fenced from front to back on the sides, she didn't have them come in through the neighbors' yards, but she knew others did. The back of her yard wasn't fenced, now open to the river. Nothing would keep Goliath in unfortunately, and of course Thaddeus could go wherever he wanted to go. Mugs was usually well-enough behaved that she didn't feel the need to fence in her property completely.

Her phone beeped a few minutes later, and there was the file from Mack. She had to love a guy who followed through when he said he would do something. As she glanced through the file, she realized it was mighty thin. *Again.* This happened a lot with these cold cases. She read what she called the CliffsNotes on it, which was the first page summary and then headed into the details. Still not very much here to go on. The local authorities had spoken to Dennis's family. They'd spoken to his friends.

Since Dennis appeared to work on the family farm, that was his place of business as well as his home. Seems the farm was so big that people took a four-wheel-drive truck to reach some of the other pastures and fields and such. Yet nobody had any idea what was going on about his disappearance. His bank accounts had no suspicious activities, and his credit cards weren't used again after that.

For all intents and purposes, Dennis had disappeared off the face of the earth from one moment to the next. That disappearing act was something Doreen didn't get and always made her very suspicious. It just didn't make any sense that somebody would do that. Without a body, it took seven years before any missing person was declared deceased, so estates could be settled, and Doreen imagined that, during that time, for the wife at least, life would have been very hard.

If she needed a loan or a mortgage or credit or any financing, how did you explain that your husband just walked off one day and didn't come home? Also the wife had to deal with the constant waiting, racing to the door at every sound, and seeing his face in crowds, only to have her hopes dashed each and every time. And were children involved? Wow. How did you handle that discussion with little ones?

Doreen couldn't imagine living that life, although in this particular case, maybe it would have been an easier life for this woman. Doreen didn't know what kind of relationship Dennis had had with his wife. Right now, Doreen would be happy if Mathew just walked off the face of the earth and left her alone, after signing *all* the paperwork of course. That would be one less worry on Doreen's plate, leaving her to happily solve whatever happened to Dennis.

Doreen's frustration was definitely building over Mathew's lack of cooperation regarding the divorce. She had to laugh at that because since when did Mathew ever cooperate? Up until a few months ago Doreen had basically avoided this step of getting a real divorce lawyer, until Mack and Nick had prodded her into getting her fair share. After all, Robin and Mathew had deceived Doreen into thinking she got nothing but what her car could hold. So now that she was aware of their shenanigans, she was getting frustrated that he wasn't cooperating. She shook her head. "You're being an idiot," she muttered.

Refocusing, she went back over the case file on her phone, looking to see if anything was there. Putting down her cell, she got up, grabbed her laptop, and sat back outside, so she could read the file a little more easily. After she went through the whole thing, she looked at the little bit of notes that she had written down. Not a whole lot was of any value. It was one of the skimpiest files she'd ever seen.

Frustrated, she figured that she would head to the library, as soon as she was done with her coffee, and see about gleaning whatever was available there. First, she would collate the important data that she had and then would set up a plan of action. She already knew she would have to talk to the wife. Dennis did have two sons, and they were ten and eleven at the time that he disappeared. That also got to her.

Would he have just upped and left if he cared about his sons?

Some guys just couldn't handle being a parent, and they wanted nothing to do with those responsibilities from one day to the next. Doreen knew a friend who'd been engaged to marry somebody, who was ready to have kids; but he met somebody else and, in an instant, ditched his fiancée and married this other woman he hardly knew. Doreen's husband, Mathew, had just shrugged and said indifferently, "She was better in bed."

Doreen didn't say anything to him, just wondering how it could all be so simple in his mind. She couldn't imagine Mack ever doing something like that. But then maybe she was the one being foolish. She didn't think so though. So far he'd always been an upright solid-guy material.

As she slowly put away the little bit of notes that she had, she organized her day. Library first and maybe a drive past Dennis's home without the animals and then sort out on the internet how to do a walkover and see if she could strike up a conversation with the wife.

Southeast Kelowna was massive, where properties were wide-spread and far apart. Some were large, and some were tiny, but there were also vineyards and orchards. This one, as she looked on the internet, appeared to be an orchard. And that would explain the large property too. However, she needed a better reason to stop than to ask them why the xeriscape garden was in the front yard, with a huge orchard there too.

After her second cup of coffee, she quickly packed up, and the animals got excited, but she shook her head. "Sorry, guys, we can't have you down at the library." But they looked at her so sad, she found herself promising to come home, and she would take them with her down to the Southeast Kelowna drive-by.

"We'll do that much at least," she promised them. Mugs let out several woofs, as if he understood. It was almost as if making her promise to follow through.

She smiled at him. "I promise. I promise." She quickly escaped, hating the guilt of leaving the animals behind because they loved to go out on trips with her. However, the library was a definite no for them. At the library, she liked to be as efficient as possible, except, as soon as she walked in, the librarian, one she knew well, stopped her.

"Ooh, have you got a new case?"

She winced at that. "Do you think that's the only reason I come in here?" she joked.

"Yes," the librarian replied immediately.

Doreen chuckled. "Well, maybe. I am looking into Dennis Polanski's disappearance."

The librarian stared at her for a moment. "Wow, I had forgotten about Dennis. That was quite a while ago."

"Right? It only came up because I saw the property on a drone video," Doreen shared, looking around, "and Mack mentioned he had investigated that case years ago."

The librarian nodded slowly. "Dennis just disappeared.

From one day to the next, he was gone, wasn't he?" She looked over at her in question.

Doreen nodded. "That seems to be what all the research is showing, yes. A body was never found, and there's been no sign of financial activity from him since. I want to see if his wife would be open to talking to me."

The librarian nodded. "She's really a sweetheart."

"Oh, good," Doreen replied. "Maybe it would be a little easier after all this time to answer questions."

"I'm sure she wants answers," the librarian stated. "Just go easy on her. Not everybody loses a spouse like that. The gossip was pretty rampant at the time."

Doreen winced. "Yeah, I'm not a big fan of gossip. It can ruin a lot of people."

The librarian nodded. "That's right. You've been the butt of a lot of gossip yourself."

"I know," she agreed, with an eye roll, "even though I'm just trying to help people."

At that, the librarian gave her a fat smile. "Sure, but, in helping one group of people, you're causing another group a lot of pain."

Doreen chuckled. "Yeah, and that's the group I'm okay to cause pain to." She turned to the back of the library, adding, "If you remember anything about the case or you know where to point me to anything interesting and juicy or to people who had anything to do with the family, let me know."

"Will do. Honestly I'd forgotten about it, until you brought up the name."

"Exactly, and it's one of the reasons why I'm looking into it. Somebody who just upped and disappeared should not be forgotten. Everybody deserves justice, and, in this case, we don't even know if justice is needed, so why don't we find out?"

And, with that, Doreen found an open computer and sat down and got to work. She searched for Dennis Polanski and his wife, Meredith Polanski, and found almost nothing. There were some mentions of the husband and wife when older people in the family died, so Doreen found some obituaries of another generation that mentioned Dennis and Meredith.

She assumed that the families had been here a long time. But again those were questions that she would have to ask Meredith. Doreen pulled up the cold case file on her phone and double-checked the names, and, sure enough, Meredith's grandmother had passed away.

Armed with that, Doreen got up, walked back over to the librarian. "I found little-to-no information on any of the family."

The librarian nodded. "I was trying to do a little bit of the research myself to see if we had anything, but really it's a fairly new concept to put old info online," she shared apologetically. "And honestly, if Dennis left on his own, he did a heck of a job, and, if he didn't leave on his own, somebody else did a heck of a job."

Doreen winced at that. "Isn't that the truth," she muttered. "Okay, I'll have to see if the wife has anything to say."

"Just remember to be nice."

"I wasn't planning on *not* being nice," Doreen stated, looking back at the librarian. "It's not really my style."

"I know, but some of these cases are still touchy issues for people."

Doreen pondered that as she headed home.

Chapter 7

AS SOON AS Doreen got home, the animals greeted her at the door. She smiled and announced, "Okay, let's go. We'll go for a drive and then have a long walk up in Southeast Kelowna, because this property apparently includes an orchard." With that, harnesses on both of the four-legged ones and the two-legged one on her shoulder, she headed back out to her vehicle. Mugs was super excited to be out on a road trip and barked several times, just happy to be tagging along.

She smiled at him. "You would make a great trucker's friend," she noted. "You're always happy to be out and about." He woofed at her several more times, as she pulled out of the driveway and headed to the area in question. She'd looked it up on her GPS, but it wasn't hard to find. She passed the little grocery store that she'd been in once before and headed on farther. It was a little harder to determine when she'd hit the right place though because these huge properties had long driveways but not a whole lot else.

She slowed when she came up to the area that she thought she was supposed to be looking for, and she noted an open gate and the name *Hillcrest Farms* etched on the side. She nodded to herself. The farm name had been in the file. "That seems likely." She got off to the side of the road and studied the area. Mugs started to bark and bark and bark. She looked over at him. "What's the matter, buddy?"

He kept on barking. She sighed. "Well, it doesn't look like a good area where we can casually walk by and stop to talk to her. So we may just drive down the driveway and see if anybody's home." She was a little hesitant to do that, considering she hadn't gotten any information to ask very much of Meredith, but, hey, if Doreen didn't try, she wouldn't get anywhere.

And, with that thought, while Mugs caterwauled the whole way, Doreen drove up to the front door at the end of the driveway. There she hopped out and studied the layout of the house and the property and a big shed on a back portion. She was surprised that she could walk right up to the house so easily. Thankfully the gate had been open.

As she studied the area, a small tractor slowly pulled around from behind the house. The small machine was dragging big fruit boxes on a trailer. Doreen watched in amazement, as it came up to the fence and stopped and then shut off. A woman hopped out, walked over, and asked, "Can I help you?"

"I'm looking for Meredith," Doreen replied.

The woman nodded. "Well, you found her. What can I do for you?"

Doreen hesitated.

Meredith frowned at her. "You are the one who came here. If you've got something to say, say it."

"My name is Doreen."

"Great, and I should care why?" Meredith asked briskly.

Trying to remember how the librarian had mentioned

how this woman was a sweetheart, Doreen added, "It's a little awkward to explain why I'm here."

Meredith stopped, hands on her hips, and suggested, "Why don't you just spit it out? If you're trying to sell something, the answer is *absolutely no way*." She turned back to her tractor.

"I'm not trying to sell anything, but I was looking into your husband's disappearance."

Meredith froze and slowly pivoted to ask, "Why?"

And such a blunt honesty filled her tone and her facial expression—just curiosity instead of grief or anything else—so Doreen replied, "Because it's what I do."

Meredith stared at her. "What are you? Some kind of amateur detective or something?"

Doreen thought about it and then nodded. "I guess you could say that."

At that, Mugs started to bark from the passenger seat in the car.

"You can let the dog out. He probably has to go to the bathroom," Meredith said. "I don't know why people drive around with dogs like that and then expect them to not want out."

"I didn't want to impose," Doreen shared.

"Well, you already are, so what difference does it make?"

Not sure what to say to that, Doreen quickly walked over, opened up her vehicle, and Mugs jumped out. She grabbed his leash, just as he was about to run around the tractor.

Meredith waved at her. "Just let him go."

"Are you sure?"

"Sure, I'm sure. We are a farm. We have dogs, animals all over the place."

Doreen let Mugs go but kept Goliath on a leash. When he sauntered forward, Meredith frowned.

"A cat on a leash? How does that work?" she asked.

"Sometimes very well," Doreen admitted, "and lots of times not very well."

Meredith burst out laughing. "Well, that's honest. If you'd told me that it works like a charm, I wouldn't have trusted another word out of your mouth."

Doreen chuckled. "You can't ever make any certainties when it comes to a cat." She shook her head. "Still, Goliath is very good-hearted and does a lot of good works, helping me solve crimes."

At that, Meredith snorted. Then she caught sight of Thaddeus, as he poked his head out from behind Doreen's hair and cried out, "Big Guy, Big Guy, Big Guy."

Doreen looked around and asked, "Do you have a parrot or anything here?"

"No," Meredith said, "but I have a couple hawks." And, sure enough, over to the side in a big cage were several hawks, now crowing.

Doreen asked, "Do you use them on the farm?"

"They're rescues," Meredith noted. "I've always run a bit of a rescue here, and, when I get them to a certain stage, they can move over to a different rescue that helps rehab them."

"Oh, that's interesting," Doreen replied, fascinated. "I never really think of other animals that need to be rescued."

Meredith shrugged. "I've always been partial to these kinds of birds." She studied Thaddeus. "Now I know who you are," but there was a note of resignation to her tone, instead of recognition.

Doreen nodded. "It might make it a little easier to explain what I do if you do understand who I am," she shared, "but I have to admit, it's not always easy."

"I'm quite surprised that you are here though. My husband went missing a long time ago."

"And you've never had any follow-up information? Nothing in all that time?"

Meredith shook her head. "No, he said goodbye to me, walked out the door, and that was it." Her voice caught at that, reassuring Doreen that Meredith cared to some extent.

"I'm sorry," Doreen muttered. "That had to be hard."

"I think the hardest part was the frustration of never getting any answers." She looked at her. "Do you really think you can get answers?" she asked curiously.

Doreen nodded. "I think so. At least I hope so. I've not done too badly so far."

"Sure, but at one point you'll run up against *that* case," Meredith stated. "I had always believed in faithfulness and loyalty and ending up in matching rocking chairs on the porch in our nineties, and then this happened, and I just don't know what to think anymore," she shared in a casual tone. "I figured he'd run off the road—because our property has several pastures and such, which requires a truck to get to them all. Then we found his vehicle."

"That part was curious, wasn't it? The truck wasn't far from here, was it?"

Meredith pointed back down the road that Doreen had come up. "No, it was just down there, only a mile or so."

"Interesting. What were the road conditions at that time?"

"It was a spring day. Absolutely no road conditions to even worry about. We can get a lot of icy roads, but it was an April day. Not much snow on the hills, nothing out of the ordinary." Meredith fisted her hands on her hips and glared.

"All in all, no reason as far as I could tell for any of this to have happened."

"And it's important to understand seemingly irrelevant things like that as well," Doreen added. "Just because it happened doesn't mean that everybody has an understanding of why or how."

"In this case nobody knew anything," Meredith muttered. "And believe me. A lot of people looked sideways in my direction, but what was I supposed to say? He was gone, and all those years I put into our marriage were also gone." She shook her head. "Still, sometimes all I really want is answers. Closure of some kind."

"I guess you don't expect him to be coming home anytime?"

Meredith studied Doreen. "I don't see how it's even possible. If he left on his own, then he can bet I don't want to see his sorry face again," she declared in a hard voice.

"That's a weird way to walk away from somebody."

"It's one thing if you get divorced, and you know where the other person is, and you know what happened—at least sometimes you know what happened—but this?" She stopped and frowned at Doreen.

"He just walked out? Nothing suspicious at the time?"

"Yeah, just left like normal and then nothing. If he arranged this, willfully, willingly, then I don't want anything to do with him. I would be happy to divorce him and to be done with this."

Doreen had to agree. "I'm going through a divorce right now myself, and it's not the easiest."

"There's no such thing as *easy* when it comes to a divorce," Meredith stated. "Compared to his disappearance, I think it would have been better. Regardless, the bottom line is, it's still something you have to go through. Even when you do go through it, you keep thinking that it will be over, and then you'll be fine, but in this case? There is no *over*. There is no *fine*. I mean, look at you now. You just show up out of the blue, and you bring it all back."

"I am sorry for that. But there's no other option if I want answers for you."

"I was having a good morning, until you showed up."

Doreen stared at her.

Meredith shrugged. "Now I'll be upset for the rest of the day, as I once again run through in my mind if I said anything, if I did anything, if I could have done something more to stop this from happening. Was there something I was supposed to do, something I could have done?" The glare that Meredith sent to Doreen stunned her. "It's those kinds of thoughts that kill you."

"I'm sorry," Doreen said. "I wasn't trying to bring back all those ugly memories."

"Well, too bad because you did." Meredith groaned and ran her hands through her hair, pulling it back off her face with more force than necessary, "But whatever, you're here now. So I presume you have questions."

Doreen nodded. "Yeah, I do, but I just really wanted to confirm the information that I had before."

"You mean, to compare what I said before to what I might say now and catch me out in a lie?" she asked in a wry tone.

"Not at all. I just don't want to be working on assumptions and find out later, had I just double-checked with you, it would be a different story."

Meredith sighed. "The police were here, and they did what they could, … but it wasn't as if they did a whole lot.

None of us could have imagined this, and, even if we could have, I don't think anybody would have expected it."

"Was he a good father?"

Meredith nodded. "He was a good father. He was one of the best at farm management. He was a good provider," she relayed, her tone short. "As far as I know, we had a good marriage, but, if he walked away willfully, then obviously I was in the dark about so much. So much so that … I don't know."

Doreen winced. "You're right. That would be one of the hardest parts."

"Of course it is. What else do you want to ask?"

Obviously Meredith was willing to help but also needed to have this over with. Doreen thought about it and repeated, "There was absolutely no follow-through afterward?"

"No. None," Meredith confirmed. "I never heard from him again. Our bank accounts weren't touched, other than by me. There was absolutely nothing as far as a money trail or even a physical trail. He literally just dropped off the face of the earth." And such bitterness filled her voice.

"What about your sons?"

"What about my boys?" Meredith stiffened. "I don't want you talking to them at all. I don't even want you near them. Took forever for them to start sleeping through the night again, and, although they're adults now, I don't want all that upset brought back."

Doreen hesitated and then nodded. "That's fine. It just might help if I got their impression of what life was like during that time period."

"They were kids. They won't know anything," she snapped. "I won't condone your looking into this if you'll bother my children."

Doreen backtracked. "I wasn't planning on it at all." However, mentally she thought, *But now I want to.* She smiled at Meredith. "How was the financial scenario at the time?"

"Ugly. We're farmers, so it's always ugly," she muttered. "Even now, the bills are high, the yields poor, the prices at my end won't be great, but you, as the consumer, will pay though the nose," she shared, with a hard laugh. "Farming isn't something you do because you'll make money," she explained. "Farming is something you do because it's what you love. It's in your blood. You are the boss and don't answer to anyone else. You get great freedom, and yet I am tethered to the land and the animals. You don't get sick days on a farm, or ice days either. Yet I do it because I love it. I love being out in the open air. I love being my own boss and working in the fields."

"Is this what you've always done?" Doreen asked curiously.

Meredith gave a one-arm shrug. "More or less, yes."

"Are you part of one of the old families in town here?"

Meredith nodded. "Yes, the farm was part of my grandfather Johnson's inheritance, whereby I also inherited a section of it when I got married, and then, when Johnson dies, I will receive another portion of it, as will with my father Danny," she shared.

"So it's yours, not Dennis's?"

"It stays with my family, my blood kin, not anybody who marries into the family. So, yeah. Even if my husband had lived, he couldn't have taken part of it away with him in the event of a divorce or separation," she explained. "It was all in trust to ensure that the family farming continued."

"Was your husband a happy farmer?"

Meredith considered that. "I wondered about that. Lots of times he was happy to get up and to go do what needed to be done, but, like all of us, lots of days he didn't want to get out of bed."

Doreen winced. "Yeah, that's more or less my morning."

Meredith laughed. "Right. It's just what happens on a farm. Even with all the machinery, it still takes human sweat and tears. Some days are good. Some days are bad, but there are always animals to be fed and always the sunrise to see and that first cup of coffee in the morning." She smiled as she looked back at the property behind the house. "Those are the things that I relish every day. Speaking of which, I have more things to do, and I can't just stand here and waste time. So hopefully you can go do something useful and find out what happened to him."

"Do you want to talk to him if I do find him?"

Meredith stopped and stared. "Seriously?" she asked.

Doreen shrugged. "It's just a question."

"Yeah, I would want to talk to him," she replied, "and then I want to beat the guy up because, if I'm talking to him, it means he left on his own, and believe me. That won't make me very happy." And, with that, she turned on the tractor, and it made so much ruckus, that ended any further questions.

Chapter 8

DOREEN DROVE DOWN to the end of the property, or at least to the next big fence, parked, and got out with the animals and slowly wandered up and down the road. She wanted to get an idea of the lay of the land, and she would spend some time on Google when she got back home. She knew roughly where the vehicle had been found, and that was her next place to visit. So after a twenty-minute walk with the animals, she got back into the car and drove farther down the road to a series of driveways leading to an intersection of country roads, and, according to the picture that she had from Mack's file, this was where the vehicle had been found. And yet it was just at an intersection of several other properties.

The whole area was secluded—no cameras, traffic lights, crosswalks, nothing. Country roads. *Was it even possible to hide a disappearance like that?*

It was pretty amazing to even think of a vehicle coming down this far, stopping, somebody getting out and then gone forever. The only reasons to get out were if they broke down, took a bathroom break, met somebody, planned to do a transfer at the time, or so that they could somehow get away from whatever it was that Dennis was trying to get away from, plus hide his tracks.

As she stood here, a vehicle drove by. It stopped and slowly backed up. She watched as an older man got out and walked toward her, his expression puzzled. "Are you all right? Do you need a hand?"

"I'm fine, thank you." She smiled at him. "However, I appreciate your stopping."

He nodded. "It's a sad world when we have to appreciate the fact that people take a moment to just be decent."

"Isn't that the truth," she muttered.

He studied her and her animals and nodded. "You're starting to get quite a name for yourself."

She winced. "It used to be easy to go around town, when people didn't know who I was."

He laughed. "Maybe, but, once you start doing this kind of stuff, and you succeed at it, that's the amazing part. It's the success rate you have. Everybody else just wants to keep track of what you're up to." He looked at the intersection and nodded once more. "You're not looking into Dennis Polanski's disappearance, are you?"

She smiled. "I was considering it. Not sure there's a whole lot to look into."

"Unless you're trying to blow your lovely record," he teased, "then this would be one to ignore. There's been no sign of him since that day. Talk about a weird case."

"I just spoke to his wife," Doreen shared, with a nod. "There doesn't appear to be any change in the situation since Dennis disappeared."

"Nope, no sign of him in all this time. I mean, good chance he's dead." And then he frowned and asked, "Don't you think?"

"That would be the instant thought that would come to mind," Doreen confirmed. "The question is, what happened to him? And, if he did leave the area, did he go willingly?"

"And yet that's about the only thing that you could say. Did he go willingly?" he repeated. "His truck was here. The only thing we could think of is that he just met somebody here, left the vehicle, and took off. We all thought he came up with somebody better than his wife. But now, after so long, we all assumed he was in Timbuktu or dead."

"How was their marriage?" she asked.

"Like all marriages, some days were good, and some days weren't. Farmers generally go to bed with the chickens and get up with the chickens," he stated, "but Dennis had other plans in life. He wanted to do more things in life. So I'm not sure that farming was a good fit for him."

"Meaning that he would be out at hours that most farmers weren't?"

He looked at her, smiled, and said, "Very perceptive."

"Was he out with anybody in particular?"

"Not that I know of," the stranger said cautiously. "Plus, it feels wrong to talk about the man like this."

"Maybe. Still, when a man's been missing for this long, if people don't talk, we'll never get answers."

"That is a viable point," he agreed. "Still feels weird though."

"Well, if you think of anything"—she pulled out a couple cards that she kept in her pocket—"can you call me, please? It will take people talking before this will get solved."

"But that would imply that people are involved."

She smiled at him. "Do you really think that somebody would take off in this day and age and stay hidden all this time and nobody would know? That nobody helped?"

He pondered that. "I suppose it's possible that somebody knows, but chances are they don't know what they know."

"Oh, now *that* I would agree with totally. The number of times that people have a little bit of information, and they don't even realize how important it is," she noted, "is massive. And then it's just one little puzzle piece for me that I can finally put together and make everything make sense."

"I'm not sure there's anything to tell you. At the time it was all the gossip because everybody had lots to say," he mentioned, with a wave of his hand, "but now, over time, there's really not much to add. He's gone, and sometimes it makes you wonder if you shouldn't just let sleeping dogs lie."

"Maybe, but what if he, the sleeping dog, didn't intend to stay as a sleeping dog?" she whispered.

"You're back to thinking that maybe he was killed?" he asked. "Believe me. We all wondered about it at the time. I mean, how could we not? But there was absolutely no proof, no evidence, no body."

"Well, there was no body *found*," she clarified, "but that's a totally different story."

He nodded at that. "You're right there. With you on the case, it'll be interesting to see how you get on." And, with that, he smiled and said, "I'm grateful that you're not stuck in a ditch here."

"Me too." She chuckled. "Thanks for stopping."

He walked back over to his truck and then he stopped and turned and shrugged. "Dennis was pretty sweet on one of the people who worked down at the post office. I often wondered if she knew anything about it."

"Did she stay behind?"

"She did, indeed, and that was one of the things that I

wondered too, until I saw her. She was kind of teary-eyed over the whole thing, and I think she really cared, but that doesn't mean that they were having an affair," he added quickly.

"No, it doesn't," Doreen agreed. "Do you have a name?"

He pondered that and then shrugged. "I guess there's no point in hiding it, as somebody will tell you. Her name was Lilly Anne."

Doreen smiled at that. "I will see if I can track her down."

"You won't have to track her far. She lives right beside the post office."

"Oh, now that's helpful." She glanced back down the road.

"Yeah, it's a big brown house off to the side. You can't miss it."

"Good, thank you for that." As he disappeared, she slowly wandered back to her vehicle. A ladylove always added to the mystery. And yet there was no mention of her in the police file. And, of course, nobody ever wanted to consider that somebody else was in Dennis's life, although apparently a lot of people had known about the tryst. Was it something gone wrong? And if something did go wrong, was it with the wife or with the lover?

Chapter 9

PARKED AT THE local store, Doreen walked in, grabbed a coffee to-go, and stepped back out with the hot coffee in her hand. She let the animals out of the vehicle and slowly wandered the neighborhood. She'd been in this area before, where she'd met Bernard. Maybe she would phone him and check to see if he knew anything about this case. He certainly seemed to know a lot of people up here. Still, when she did that, it seemed to perturb Mack.

She wandered toward the post office, and, sure enough, a house was next door. On the gate, a sign read Lilly Anne's Place.

Doreen hesitated and then shrugged and, with the animals in tow, walked up to the front door. The door opened before she ever had a chance to knock.

A woman, maybe in her late forties, stared at her.

"Hi. My name is Doreen."

"Yeah, I know who you are." She motioned at the animals. "They are a dead giveaway."

She nodded. "So I'm finding out."

Lilly Anne chuckled. "If you ever wanted to hide who you are, you would have to walk around without them."

"I'm not trying to hide who I am," Doreen replied, "and sometimes my animals help to get answers."

"Answers seem to be what you're always out and about to get, so why are you here?"

"I'm wondering if I can do anything to help solve"—she took a deep breath—"Dennis Polanski's disappearance."

"Good Lord," Lilly Anne exclaimed. "I always wondered if anybody would care enough to open that case."

It was Doreen's turn to look surprised. "Well, it's not as if the police didn't try."

"I know they did, and they talked to me at the time. In fact, they talked to everybody up here."

"But did they talk to you in terms of being a special friend to Dennis?" Doreen asked.

Lilly Anne paled. "I don't know where you got that information from," she replied stiffly, "However, I won't sit here and be treated as if I was some sort of cheap affair."

"Absolutely not. I did not mean it that way. I intended that question solely for the purpose of clarification," Doreen explained. "Yet you must understand that, over time, some people will remember things differently, and your name came up in a discussion I had earlier."

"Of course it did," she muttered. "I was always really good friends with Dennis. We could talk. Did I care for him? Yes. Absolutely I loved him to bits, and, if he had told me that he was leaving his wife and then asked if I was interested, it would have been a flat-out *absolutely*," she declared, staring right at Doreen. "But I never had an affair with him, and I wouldn't have because he's a married man, and that's not the type of person I am."

Oh really? Doreen smiled at her, not believing a word she said. The woman kept clenching her hands as she spoke about not having an affair. "That would have been hard too," she murmured. "To have known that this guy just up and left from one day to the next."

"That was the thing. Everybody assumed he left. I just didn't see it happening."

"If that's the case, what do you think happened?"

"I think somebody killed him," she stated bluntly, and, with that, she stepped back inside and slammed the door.

Chapter 10

BACK HOME AGAIN, Doreen pondered the little bit she'd learned. It made sense that Dennis had met his demise by somebody else's hand, but Doreen wasn't quite sure that was her conclusion yet.

Now, figuring out who else was involved or who else might know something? *That* would be the challenge.

When it came to cold cases like this, Doreen needed somebody who cared, not somebody who just wanted to have it all go away. Just then an idea came to her, and she pulled out her phone. Still, she hesitated, wondering if Meredith would even talk to her. And could she find a number, that was a different story. Although it didn't take long, she found a number in the local phone book. Deciding to find out just how cooperative Meredith was, Doreen quickly dialed her.

Without even saying hello, Meredith asked, "Who's there?"

Doreen winced. "Hey, sorry to bother you, this is Doreen again."

There was silence on the other end, and then her tone was hard but resigned. "*Great*," Meredith muttered. "So I guess, this will just continue to be my life?"

Doreen sighed. "If I can find answers without asking you questions, … I would do that, but that's not possible in this case."

"So what is it then?" she snapped. "I'm busy."

And Doreen knew that she was and that was a legitimate argument. It was also a sign of just how stressed Meredith was. "Did he have any health issues?" Doreen asked.

A snort came on the other end. "Of all the things that I expected you to ask, that's not one of them."

"I need to know if he would walk away for any reason, potentially leaving you in a better position than to watch him die. Or was something else going on? Or was there a life insurance policy?"

"Even if there was a life insurance policy," Meredith noted caustically, "without a body, I certainly can't access it."

"No, but then some people like to do a long con," Doreen explained, her tone cool. "So is it possible to get an answer, please?"

"No, as far as I understood, there was no health issue," she replied abruptly. "He was also the self-serving kind of person who wouldn't do that. If anything, he would want to lock me down to ensure he would be well cared for."

"So he was selfish?"

"Very. Doesn't mean I didn't love him, but I certainly knew who he was." And, with that, she added, "Now I have to get back to work." And she quickly disconnected.

It was such an interesting comment for her to make and yet it revealed an awful lot about their relationship, plus confirming Doreen's initial understanding of the man involved. For a moment she wondered if he could have had a brain aneurism or a sudden psychotic episode.

These things happened, not very often, but it certainly wasn't out of the realm of possibility. However, if he didn't have any health issues that anybody knew about, then that would stave off him making that kind of personal sacrifice of saving Meredith the years of torment of watching him slowly decline. Doreen almost laughed at the fanciful idea.

She knew some people out in the world felt that way and did things like that to help others, but, so far, she hadn't heard anybody say anything along those lines about Dennis. Meredith Polanski was not uncooperative, but not exactly a grieving widow either. And again not terribly suspicious, considering that she was carrying on a farm on her own, maybe implying that he had left to get away from her. Also not something that Doreen wanted to even look at.

Life insurance was an interesting thing. Would it pay out if there were no body? Would it pay out even if he was declared legally dead? More to the point, was there even a life insurance policy on Dennis? Meredith had not clarified that matter either. Doreen wondered who would know. She didn't think she knew anybody in the insurance industry, and, even if she did know, was it something that they would freely give out information on, or was it something they would hold close to their chest in order to stop people from trying to do away with their spouses?

Just even the thought of doing something like that made her cringe—but then again she had had enough of Mathew's shenanigans and wouldn't be at all unhappy if he got hit by a car. She stopped and closed her eyes.

"Oh, wow, Doreen, that is so not you. Just because you've been through a lot with him doesn't mean that you want to wish him ill will." Sure, it was a lovely fleeting thought that would free her from all this headache and paperwork, but, considering they were at the stage of the game where he was ready to walk away and to release her from all of this, it was hardly appropriate.

Chastising herself for being that *B* word that she refused to say out loud, she wandered out to the backyard and stood on the patio, feeling a little bit out of sorts. She really needed information.

Just then her phone rang. She looked down to see Millicent calling. "Hi, Millicent. Everything okay?"

"Oh, it is," she began, but her tone was frightful. "An awful lot of weeds are here."

"Oh, dear," Doreen muttered, wincing slightly. "Do you want me to come and pull a bunch for you?" She knew that Millicent got quite perturbed when the weeds took over, and she just didn't have the mobility to go out there and tackle them herself.

Millicent hesitated. "I hate to ask. I know you're so busy."

"I'm not that busy," Doreen replied. "I'm kind of in-between cases."

At that, Millicent laughed, a bit more relaxed. "But not for long, I'm sure."

Such an affectionate admiration filled her tone that Doreen had to smile. "I'll come, and, if nothing else, I'll get these weeds that are bothering you, and we'll go from there."

"That would be absolutely wonderful if you could do that," Millicent murmured.

"When do you want me to come?" Millicent hesitated, and Doreen smiled. "I gather right now?"

"It doesn't have to be right now," Millicent rushed, "but I guess the sooner, the better would help me to know that these are taken care of."

"No problem," Doreen said. "Give me a little time to get changed and go to the bathroom, and then I'll walk on over."

"Oh, lovely. I really do appreciate this."

"I know you do," Doreen agreed cheerfully. "Besides, the animals would be happy to get in a good walk and to visit with you."

"Oh, and I do hope you bring them," she said. "It's always so nice to see them."

Smiling, Doreen nodded. "Don't worry. We'll be on our way soon." And, with that, she went into the house, washed up, changed, and was ready. Outside, she headed in the direction of Millicent's place, the animals trotting happily at her side. Even Thaddeus was walking today. Doreen's mind was still busy, wondering about this new cold case. It would take her a little bit to get sorted through it. However, she needed a thread or two to pull first, something to sort through. In this case, it was becoming increasingly obvious that whoever had pulled this off had done so very efficiently and with great ease, and that kind of scared her.

She just wanted to believe everybody could get along, and, as she was quickly becoming aware, that was a naïve attitude.

Her husband had always said that she was innocent of the world. At the time she had just nodded because what else could she say? Only now did she realize that, in many ways, she really was, becoming less so every day, but still very much somebody who didn't have any worldly experience and didn't know the true face of reality. She lacked *worldly experience*, yes, yet at a level where she didn't have to worry about anything. She knew what was going on in her world, and she had people around her who had dealt with all the problems and had made life simple and easy for her.

Not at all what was happening right now. She had grown up over the last six months or so and was more certain of herself, and she'd been free and clear to make her own choices and to see reality for herself. For that she could certainly thank her ex. When she had been with Mathew, he had kept her very isolated from the goings-on around her. Not a good thing considering all she had to quickly learn, once she got out on her own.

As she walked to Millicent's, Doreen pondered the circle of events that had brought her to this point, where she was actively looking for cases, actively looking at a life where she could help others sort through these kinds of things. And, if she had enough money that she didn't have to work elsewhere, then she could continue to do it on a volunteer basis, and that was something that she had to consider too.

Do I want to get paid for something like this?

Was that even a possibility? And would it change her in some way?

When she had no money, she still did this, and so she figured that, as long as she had enough money to continue to live as she wanted and needed to, then money shouldn't even enter into the equation. If she'd done this sleuthing when she was still broke, then surely she could do it while she was well off.

And that just brought back memories of the emails from Paula, her art specialist working with Scott.

Doreen knew a lot of people would want to get paid for their efforts, but Doreen's satisfaction didn't come from earning money doing this but in finding closure for the families involved. So, if she were to charge for her sleuthing, but nobody could afford to pay her, that defeated the purpose. Doreen was trying to help others.

Although she could see the value of people who appreciated the work that she was doing, it didn't have to be monetary appreciation. It could just be words of gratitude. She wasn't doing it to get paid, and she really didn't want other people to think that either. Even now, without getting paid, just listening to Richard and how he sees her as a busybody, made Doreen shake her head. Sometimes with those kind of comments and those near-death experiences Doreen had encountered all too often with these cases, she had to wonder why she was doing it.

She knew Mack wondered why she risked her life for these cases too.

Chapter 11

THE WALK TO Mack's mother's house was calm and uneventful, and, upon reaching Millicent's place, she walked around to the back to find the older woman already sitting on the deck, waiting. Mugs immediately raced toward her, greeting her as a long-lost friend. Even Goliath wrapped around her legs a few times. Thaddeus hopped up onto her table and squawked, "Thaddeus is here. Thaddeus is here!"

Millicent burst out laughing and beamed when she saw Doreen bringing up the rear. "There you are. It's so lovely to see you." She bent a little lower to stroke Goliath's back and scratch under Mug's chin before straightening to give Thaddeus a gentle head butt.

Doreen wondered if this was all just a chance to have some company, in which case she'd have to get the brothers to come and visit their mother more often. As it was, Doreen took care of the gardens and charged Mack for her services. With a half smile at the older lady, she replied, "Hey. How are you doing today?"

"I'm not too bad," Millicent declared, smiling broadly. "Thank you for asking."

"At least it wouldn't be too bad if those pesky weeds

would stop bugging you, *huh*?"

Millicent chuckled. "I try hard not to let them bother me, but, every time I see them, I get upset."

"The more you try *not* to look," Doreen agreed, with a knowing nod, "that just means that they'll be there in your face all that much more."

"How does that work anyway?" Millicent asked, staring at her.

"Because you keep trying to *not* see them, and the more you try *not* to see them, the more you see them. That's what happens to me too. Remember that saying, *Don't think about an elephant?*"

"I'm sure the psychologists would have a reason for that too." Millicent chuckled.

"They do. It puts the suggestion in your mind and you can't not think about the dratted things. But it's good enough to know that basically the weeds are there to torment us. So, as long as you'll get tormented, they'll keep coming and bugging you."

Millicent nodded. "Well, thank heavens I have a weed doctor to come and fix them."

"Ah, is that what I am now? Seems that everybody has a lot of names for me."

"I'm sure they do. Not everybody solves mysteries the way you do though," Millicent stated. "You have no idea how envious I am."

Doreen asked, "Why envy?"

"Because you're young enough to do this," she explained. "In my day, women weren't supposed to do anything."

Doreen snorted. "Yeah, that's still in our day too. That would have been my ex's wish."

Millicent nodded. "There's a certain amount of, you know, … *women can't do stuff* nonsense, and I always felt that was such a shame. But you, my dear, you keep breaking all the norms."

"Whether people like it or not," Doreen quipped, with a nod.

"Keep doing it," Millicent declared. "It's good for the men."

At that, Doreen burst out laughing. "You mean, for Mack and me?"

Millicent gave her a bright smile. "I would love to have you join the family."

Doreen's face flushed. "Well, that was a little bit too honest," she muttered.

"No, not at all. I'm not getting any younger, and neither is that boy of mine." She sighed. "Neither of my boys are," she added, with a note of disgust. "You would think I would have grandchildren by now."

Doreen winced because this conversation was not the way she wanted it to go. "I think they'll have to work that out themselves."

"Oh, I know. I know. That doesn't mean I wouldn't like to push them along that path though," she said, vexed.

Doreen gave her a smile. "It might be better to leave them to work it out on their own though."

"Maybe, but they aren't doing a very good job of it," Millicent shared, with a huff. "I mean, I came into this late, but I certainly didn't expect them to, as well."

At that, Doreen laughed at her. "You got to make your choices back then, and they get to make theirs now."

"I know. I know. I know," she grumbled. "However, being so much older as a parent, it was good in the sense that

I was mature and could understand a lot more things than I might have if I had been a much younger mother," she explained. "Still, I do find now, because I am that much older, that I'm very much looking for these grandkids all that much faster."

"Which is hardly fair to your sons," Doreen reminded her.

"I understand, and I'm not trying to be unfair to them. However, I don't really feel like being fair." And she gave her a bright grin. "So maybe you should just tell Mack to hurry up."

Doreen chuckled. "Nope. I know perfectly well why Mack's taking as long as he is, and it's at my request. So he'll have to wait just a little bit longer."

At that, Millicent looked at her glumly. "Haven't got rid of that man yet?"

"Oh, I keep hoping," Doreen replied, with a bright smile. "Now, how about these weeds?" At that, Millicent fell to explaining the weeds that were really bothering her. As Doreen stood here on the side of the patio, she could see the worst of them clearly. "Funny how they like to grow where we can't quite reach them," she noted, as she got down and could spy the weeds poking out among the roses.

"If I wasn't having so much trouble getting up and down, I would have tried."

"No, no, not needed," Doreen replied. "I've got this." And she went at the weeds, as Millicent pointed them out. Doreen made sure to rip them out of the ground, taking the roots with them. Mugs grabbed several in fun and gave them big shakes sending dirt flying everywhere, unfortunately covering Goliath who swiped at it.

Thaddeus chortled watching the other two. Doreen just

shook her head and dug in. By the time she had worked for a good hour, she realized quite a few had been here. "I don't know how they grew this fast," she shared. "I was just here a week ago."

"I know. *Right*? That's part of the reason why I hated to call you back again, but I know Mack upped the watering, since we recently got that bout of sunshine and heat. So the garden's just growing like crazy."

"I haven't even bothered to check out the status on my own garden," Doreen admitted, looking back at Millicent. "This just reminds me. I need to do weeding like this when I get home."

Millicent nodded. "It gets away from us so quickly," she replied, as she leaned over and pointed out another one. Doreen quickly snagged it and then several more. When she thought she had every weed gone—at least those Millicent could see—Doreen stepped up and stood behind the older lady and looked at the garden. "I'm not seeing too much else. How about you?"

Millicent looked around and nodded. "I think that's got to be it, but you know they're suckers. So, they'll be back."

"They will, indeed," Doreen agreed, "but so will I. Therefore, it's not a problem."

Millicent reached over and patted her hand. "You're a good girl, and I really appreciate you for humoring an old woman like me."

"I'm not humoring you," Doreen replied. "I understand perfectly well what it's like to have weeds that you can't get at and being frustrated because of the physical constraints that you have to deal with."

"It's no fun getting old," Millicent remarked, "particularly when you can see that there'll be all these years that you'll miss out on because your sons are taking their sweet time starting families."

Knowing they were walking right back into that dangerous territory, Doreen smiled and pointed toward her home. "Now, if there are no more weeds to sort out, I will walk my animals home."

"Really?" Millicent asked. "I was hoping you would have tea."

Doreen hesitated and then smiled. "How about a fast cuppa?"

Millicent brightened and went in to put on the teapot. In truth, Doreen hadn't had a chance to ask her about the missing Dennis, and she should; Millicent might even have known him. When she came out a little bit later with the teapot in hand, Doreen kept working on the errant weeds until she sat down and then asked, "Do you know anything about the missing Dennis Polanski case?"

Millicent frowned. "Wow, that's a name I hadn't heard in a long time."

"I just wondered if there was anything I could do to help the family with their missing husband and father," Doreen shared. "I came upon the property on an odd drone footage, and Mack told me that the owner of the property had just upped and disappeared."

"Oh my, that does take me back." She shook her head. "Who would have thought that even something like that was possible?"

"I certainly wouldn't have," Doreen admitted, with a nod. "You think about things like that, and you don't really see how somebody could have managed to disappear quite so completely."

"Exactly," Millicent agreed. "I mean, in this day and age,

the police have so many methods of tracking down a person that you would think they would have found him by now." She looked over at Doreen. "I think it's a great idea that you're looking into it," she declared. "That family must be so sad, wondering what happened to him."

"They are. I did talk to the wife," Doreen noted her gaze going over Millicent's yard to see Mugs and Goliath stretched in the sun close but not touching, just snoozing the morning away. Even Thaddeus had taken up roost on the railing snoozing. "I'm not sure at this point in time that she's wondering as much as she's just vexed by it all."

"Vexed?" Millicent repeated. "If it were my husband, I would be devastated."

"And that was an easy thing for me to jump to a criticism, thinking that maybe she didn't care or maybe she even had something to do with Dennis's disappearance. However, after all these years, she's probably just as upset about the fact that there's been no closure, and potentially that's all it was—just a reaction."

Millicent sat here for a long moment. "I guess you really do learn a lot about human nature in these investigations, don't you?"

"It certainly helps." Doreen chuckled. "We can have all kinds of ideas and still be very wrong, and you don't want the wrong idea to be something that you're so married to that you refuse to look at everything else."

Millicent nodded. "I guess for me, the question is why."

"Exactly," Doreen agreed, with a smile. "If he left on his own, why? And, if somebody decided to kill him or remove him or whatever they did, there still has to be a motivation. And, if there's motivation, how on earth do we find out what it was?"

Millicent stared at her for a long moment. "There were rumors that he was having an affair."

"Right." Doreen nodded. "I talked with the lady who works at the post office. Lilly Anne."

Millicent looked at her and then chuckled. "You really do like to stay on top of this stuff, don't you?"

"No point starting something if I can't look into it, and I get that, for a lot of people, I'm just being snoopy and disregarding people's feelings," she relayed, stopping to gather her thoughts. "Yet that's not why I'm doing this, plus it's not the easiest thing to question people, even this many years later, and not have them react in a bad way."

"So you did talk to Adelaide?"

She stopped and stared. "Adelaide?"

"Yes."

"Is she the woman who worked at the post office?"

Millicent frowned. "I'm not sure where she worked back then, but there was talk of an affair with Adelaide."

Doreen hesitated, then suggested, "Maybe he had affairs with more than one."

Millicent's face wrinkled up in disgust. "I wouldn't be at all surprised. If they'll take that first *walkabout*, you know that nothing will stop them from doing it twice."

"What do you know about the woman he had an affair with?" she asked.

Millicent shrugged. "I don't know a whole lot. I just know that there was talk of a woman in his life."

"Yet you called her Adelaide."

"Sure, but I don't really know … I guess that's …"

"Where would you have heard something like that, heard that woman's name?"

"Just the rumor mill."

"Well, it's that rumor mill that I need to lock down a little bit better."

Millicent smiled at her. "What about your grandmother? Are you telling me that she doesn't have all the details on this case?"

"There is a little bit of information out there, but a lot of people have forgotten about it."

"If so, that won't help you very much to make any headway. I think because Dennis was a grown man, people assumed that he may have just walked away on his own."

"Possibly," Doreen murmured. "I mean, when you think about it, if he had a reason, like another lover or somebody he wanted to start over with, then what was to keep him here?"

Millicent nodded slowly. "Adelaide did work. I thought she worked for the city." Millicent stared off into her garden.

"This woman he had an affair with?"

"Yes." Millicent turned to face Doreen. "However, I can't remember the details."

"Do you know anybody who might have had a closer connection?"

Millicent eyed her thoughtfully for a moment. "Maybe, … but I'll have to ask her if she's willing to talk to you though."

"Who would this be?" Doreen asked, puzzled. "More to that the point, would she have had something to say to the police about it?"

"I don't think so, at least not back then. She might now."

"Why's that?"

"Because I know she had an affair with him herself."

"Oh, wow, so this guy really was the one to step out on

his wife."

Millicent nodded. "I wouldn't say anything about it because I don't like to speak ill of the dead," she shared, "but I guess you do need to know if other people were in his life, don't you?"

"Absolutely," Doreen said, her tone flat, "because I hadn't read anything in the news or in the police reports about him having multiple affairs. So, that's a motive in many ways."

"But it's only a motive if the wife killed him."

"Not at all," Doreen disagreed, looking at Millicent. "A lover could have as well. Maybe she wanted Dennis to choose, and he did, and the lover was not the chosen one."

At that, Millicent blanched. "Oh, dear. I sure hope my friend didn't have anything to do with it."

Doreen waited while Millicent fought this inner demon about whether she should say something more or not. "The only way I'll know," Doreen proceeded cautiously, "is if I talk to her."

At that Millicent gave several more thoughtful frowns in her direction, as if that would help her make a decision.

Doreen waited patiently, just drinking her tea.

Finally Millicent gave a heavy sigh. "I guess I have no point in hiding it because I get you've already heard about one affair, right?"

Doreen nodded. "Although the woman did say that she didn't sleep with him."

Millicent rolled her eyes at that. "Of course she'll say that, particularly when the wife is still in town and is quite possibly living close to her."

"It's always a good motivation for staying quiet," Doreen murmured. "Yet it's also a great motivation for having something to do with his disappearance."

Millicent gasped at that. "I would be devastated if my friend had anything to do with it," she admitted. "We've been friends for a long time."

"How old is she?" Doreen asked, thinking that the ages between Adelaide and Dennis were off quite a bit here.

"Oh, she's not my age at all," Millicent explained. "She's the dearest daughter of a friend of mine, and she also had her children late in life, which is another reason why we were so close. I mean, when you're forty-five and dealing with bed-wetting toddlers and then sixty-five dealing with twenty-year-olds, you know things weren't quite so different for us. We bonded over familiar territory."

"Ah, okay, so who is this friend then?"

Millicent still hesitated.

Doreen patted her hand and whispered, "I promise I'll just talk to her. I'm not trying to accuse her of anything, but we do need to sort this out. And it's time, don't you think?" Something about that wording made Millicent nod.

"You're right. It is definitely time." She sighed. "I mean, this kind of stuff has to be dealt with before it continues, and nobody has any answers. … Her name is Adelaide. Adelaide Bonner."

"And her mother?"

"Yeah. My girlfriend Sue Ellen Bonner, her mother, passed away a few years ago, and Adelaide and I have remained quite close friends over it all."

"Lovely," Doreen noted. "Contact information?"

Millicent pulled out her phone and found her Contacts. "But you'll be gentle with her, right? I know that she was quite in love with him, and he was younger. So she always felt that was the reason that he broke off with her."

"Maybe, but he also might have been just playing the field and had too many other options."

Millicent winced. "I do hope you don't tell her that."

"No, I'm not planning on doing that." Doreen chuckled, as she finished her tea. She had the contact information for Adelaide Bonner, and Doreen would call her from home. "Now you let me know if those weeds come back and start bothering you again, okay?"

As she got up with her animals, who'd been more or less patiently waiting throughout the afternoon, Mugs started barking in excitement. "Are you guys ready to go home?"

Mugs pranced toward the sidewalk. Goliath raced ahead and threw himself down on the sidewalk in first place, while Thaddeus squawked and tried to walk up Doreen's leg. She lifted him to her shoulder and he settled right into his happy place.

Ever-so-slightly with a wistful look on her face, Millicent waved goodbye at them.

Doreen started the walk back home again and sent Mack a message. **Just leaving your mom's. She's pretty lonely.**

She got back a thumbs-up emoji, which probably meant that he would love to talk but couldn't. However, he acknowledged what she was saying, which is that he needed to spend more time with his mother.

She really did hope that Nick moved closer to town, so that he could spend some time with his mother, too. Doreen had talked to Nick and Mack about it before, and this ritual of Doreen's, texting the men after having spent time with Millicent, was becoming a habit. She didn't know exactly how old Millicent was, but it was definitely something to be considered, especially when having children late in life, then realizing you may not have the same number of years with your grandchildren that you might have wanted.

Not that it was an issue for Doreen. She didn't have anybody in her life—not anyone she was planning on having children with anytime soon.

Chapter 12

Tuesday Morning …

WHEN DOREEN WOKE up the next morning, she stretched, yawned, and rolled over, only to have Thaddeus quack right in her ear. She bolted upright in a hurry. "What are you doing here?" she asked. Thaddeus normally stayed on his roost until she got up, but right now he was hunkered down on her pillow, staring at her. She reached up and gently stroked his feathers.

He leaned into her ear and whispered, "Thaddeus loves Nan. Thaddeus loves Nan."

Doreen frowned. "I hope you love Doreen too," she replied in exasperation. His words may not have matched his actions, but she also knew from his actions that he loved her too. But, of course, Nan would take precedence in his mind. She smiled at him as she got up and asked, "Do you want to shower?"

He started cackling. "*He, he, he, he.*"

He waddled behind her into the shower. She turned on the water and stepped in, shampooing her hair before she realized that he was already behind her, tossing the water everywhere, as he preened under the shower.

She smiled at him. "I don't know if it's common for all birds like you to want showers like this, but you sure do like yours." She left the water running a little bit longer than necessary, just for his sake.

When she finally turned it off, he gave her that look.

"No, that's enough for now." She stepped out, wrapped herself up in a towel. Getting him dry was a completely different issue. She knew he could handle a lot of it himself, but he was pretty soaked. She bent down, scooped him up, and tried patting him dry for a bit. Then she perched him atop the counter and wondered how he would react to her blow dryer, whether it would be damaging to him or scary to him. She turned it on and left it on the counter just blowing off to the side.

He walked over, curious, and then stepped into the wind. He stayed like that, seemingly enjoying the hot air, but now he appeared to be a full-blown puff ball on stick legs. She chuckled, as she shut off her hair dryer. "What do you think?" she asked him.

Thaddeus started pecking away at the hair dryer, and she turned it back on again, this time trying to smooth his feathers a little bit, so that they didn't all look like he'd just had a bad hair day. He did start to preen after a few more minutes, and, before long, he was looking way better than she was. She shook her head at that. "Don't know how you manage it," she said, "but you've got that gorgeous look down pat. Some of us have to put a little more work into it."

Still chuckling, she left him alone with the blow dryer still working on him. By the time she was dressed, she walked back in to see him sitting there in front of the hair dryer, his eyes closed, just letting the heat wash over him. She turned it off, and he opened his eyes and glared at her.

"I know, but it's time to go get food."

He squawked, "Food, food, food."

"Yes, let's go get food. I'm hungry."

"I'm hungry. I'm hungry. I'm hungry."

She glared at him. "You can also stop that at any time."

Instead he chuckled. "*He, he, he, he, he.*"

"You are quite the conniving little bird, aren't you?" He eyed her, almost as if to say, *How dare she?* Yet she knew better. This guy had all kinds of tricks up his sleeve.

Down in the kitchen, the other two animals milled about, waiting for her. She gave Goliath a big scrub and then the same for Mugs. With the coffee on, the animals now tucked into their food bowls, she headed outside to the patio.

This house and her yard were still her favorite places to be. She was eternally grateful to Nan, who had made it happen. It was such a glorious space for Doreen that she constantly sat in joy. She wasn't even sure she'd said thank you enough to everybody who made her new and improved backyard happen. It had been such a pleasure to watch the men come together and do the work on her deck and her patio and the walkways, even though she'd been worried about the money at the time. She was so grateful now that she looked at the place and realized that, if she had hesitated to upgrade her yard back then, she wouldn't be anywhere near as happy right now. And she owed Mack a big thank-you for that too.

Once the coffee was done dripping, she snagged her first cup, stepped outside again, and walked down to the river. That was the other aspect of her life here that she absolutely adored, hearing the water, hearing the birds, their early morning chirps, as she sat by the river. The bench that she absolutely loved waited for her there too.

As she sat, she heard somebody next door rustling around, and she called out, "Good morning, Richard."

First came silence from the other side of the fence and then a *harrumph*, before he finally said, "Good morning."

"I hope you're having a good day."

"Maybe. … What are you up to today?"

"Hopefully not too much," she replied. "I could use some time off."

"Well, if you don't interfere in everybody's business," he replied, "I'm sure you'll get it."

She chuckled. "You could be right, but I do have another case I'm working on."

Richard grumbled. "Finding Dennis? Good luck with that."

"I know, isn't it sad?" she noted. "Although this one isn't exactly an emergency, it's another missing person from a decade ago. You were right about the time line. Just that worry that potentially somebody else had suffered way back when and the family still has no closure in all this time makes me want to help."

"What do you mean?" he asked.

She watched an almost invisible gate open up, backing onto the river, and he stepped out.

She stared at him. "Wow, I didn't even remember you had a gate at the rear of your property."

He nodded. "I rarely use it. Plus it's overgrown out here, which hides the gate too. It's pretty rusty though," he pointed out. "I probably should get it fixed." He glared at the gate, as if it were something to be despised.

She smiled. "Maybe. That way you can enjoy the water. It's really nice to come down to the river."

"I don't know why you would want that," he argued. "It's dirty."

She smiled. "It might be dirty, but it's also Mother Nature," she shared cheerfully. "For me that brings all kinds of other things into play."

He shrugged at that. "Still, it is just dirty," he repeated. He frowned at the animals. "They seem so normal today."

Grinning, she nodded. "That's because they are normal." And again he just eyed her. She winced. "I get that, in your mind, they're probably some sort of terrible invention, but they're really nice animals."

He shrugged. "As long as they don't bite me."

"Believe me. They won't." Then, right at that moment, Mugs decided to race over toward Richard, coming at a speed that he obviously wasn't comfortable with because he backed up and yelled, "Get it off, get it off me."

She sighed. "Mugs, come here. We don't need to scare him."

"I'm not scared." Richard glared at her.

She nodded and didn't respond to that. "Come on, Mugs."

Mugs stopped, then slowly walked a little bit closer, sniffing the ground where Richard had stood.

"He won't harm you," Doreen explained. "He's just trying to get to know you."

"He doesn't need to know me," Richard declared in a raspy voice. "You've caused more than enough problems around this place."

"Maybe that is some people's perception, but I've also helped in many ways, as was my intent," she stated. "I get that my methodology is different and hasn't made everybody happy, but surely it hasn't been all bad." He still glared at her. "Your brother got out of it okay," she pointed out.

"Sure," he grumbled, "but you might very well have gotten him thrown into jail for it."

"No, not him. Roscoe didn't do anything wrong," she replied, with the gentlest of smiles, "although I really am sorry about his friend."

Richard nodded stiffly. "Nobody ever likes to see the friends that he has known that long and to find out they've done something so horrible. So, for that, I do thank you." Surprised, she nodded and watched as he quickly stepped through the hidden back gate in the fence, before Mugs could follow him.

"Come on, Mugs. Leave him alone. We'll take this one step at a time." Mugs barked at her several times and then wandered back to her. And then, as if caught by the glimpse of a rabbit or something, he dashed to the water and jumped in.

She groaned. "Really? Now you'll be soaked."

But he was having way too much fun for her to try and stop him. As a matter of fact he looked like he was having an absolute ball. She smiled and just let him go, splashing water all about. He really was enjoying himself. She watched his antics for a few minutes, hearing Richard puttering around in his backyard.

Then she called out, "Do you remember anything else about Dennis Polanski's disappearance?"

First came silence, and then the rusted back gate opened cautiously. He looked at Mugs in the water, and an expression of complete distaste washed over him. "Better your house than mine," he muttered, as he watched the dog.

"Mugs will be totally fine." Doreen gave Richard a wave of her hand. "Just like us, he dries too."

He glared at her, as if she were making fun of him. Then he nodded stiffly. "I know a little bit about Dennis's case," he began, "just the same as what everybody knows."

"So you didn't personally know him?"

He shook his head. "No, I didn't know him, didn't know anything about it, but, considering the guy's truck was found just down the road," he stated, with a headshake, "that made all of us pay attention."

She pondered that. "That would be a good motive for doing it too, wouldn't it?"

"Sorry?" he asked in confusion.

"Well, if you wanted to draw attention to something, that would do it, wouldn't it? I mean, park the vehicle just a few blocks away, close enough that he could have walked home, even if he had put the truck in a ditch, and yet there's no sign of him."

"Yet it could have just meant that he transferred vehicles," Richard suggested, staring at her. "What other reasons would there be for it?"

"We don't know yet," she shared. "That's the thing about these kinds of cases. Until you get all the answers, you really are just guessing."

"I think you guess a lot," he declared in an accusatory tone.

"Maybe, and sometimes my guesses are very good." He frowned at that, but there wasn't a whole lot that he could say, considering she'd just finished dealing with Richard's brother, Roscoe, and she had come up with a lot of accurate guesses.

"Maybe," he conceded. "Still, it would be better if you had actual answers first."

"Wouldn't that be nice," she quipped in a jovial tone.

"Too bad people don't like to talk."

"Especially to strangers," Richard stated.

"What about an Adelaide Bonner?"

Richard replied, "She works down at the city."

"That's what I heard. Do you know anything about her?"

He slowly and cautiously shook his head. She just nodded, remained silent. He asked her, "Why? What's she got to do with this?"

"Maybe nothing. Again we're back to not trying to guess but to get answers. I'll go talk to her later today and see if she knows anything."

He frowned at that. "She's a nice lady," he replied stiffly.

"Good," Doreen murmured. "Maybe then she'll have a moment or two to talk to me."

"I still don't know why you want to talk to her." Richard frowned at Doreen, and the frown grew darker and stronger as he stood there.

"Maybe there's no need to talk to her, but I won't know that until I get a chance to do so."

He gave a faint nod and continued to stare at Doreen. "I wouldn't want you to upset her. She's a nice lady." And, with that, he slowly turned and retreated to his backyard.

Doreen was amused at his defense of the *nice* lady who worked in town, yet it was nice to see him caring about somebody. She pondered that, as she went back inside her house and had breakfast, wondering how she was supposed to get a hold of this woman and talk to her privately.

But just then, as she was making toast, her phone rang. It wasn't a number that she knew. She answered it. "Hello, can I help you?" she asked, as she identified herself.

"Yes, I'm Adelaide Bonner," she replied. "I suppose you

won't quit bothering me until I talk to you, so I would appreciate it if you could meet me later today, and we can have a conversation."

Recognizing the name, Doreen told her, "I can do that. I presume Millicent contacted you?"

"Yes, she felt terribly guilty about it."

Doreen chuckled. "I did tell her that I would try to be gentle."

Adelaide sighed. "Nothing quite so foolish as an old fool in love," she replied. "So I would just as soon get this over with, once and for all."

"Why don't we do lunch," Doreen offered.

Adelaide hesitated. "I don't know. … I don't really want to lose time at work. Plus I need the money, you know."

"That's fine. I can come down around your lunch hour. Why don't we just sit outside in the park and talk?"

"That would work," Adelaide replied, "if you're okay with that."

"I'm fine with that. If we sit outside in the park, I can bring the animals."

"Yes, do bring the animals," Adelaide said. "I have heard quite a bit about them."

"They're definitely characters." Then setting up the time for eleven-thirty, she rang off and then phoned Millicent back. After a bit of hello greetings, Doreen tried to put Millicent's mind at ease. "Millicent, it's all right. I'm meeting Adelaide outside in the park, and we'll talk today."

"Oh, good," Millicent replied in relief. "I have to admit I felt pretty bad about it all."

"Well, now you don't have to. She phoned me, and we'll just meet for lunch and have a quick conversation."

"Okay, I feel much better, thank you."

And, with that, Doreen ended the call and sat, wondering just how people got so involved in each other's lives that everybody had to give everybody a heads-up, especially when Doreen was only trying to contact them. As she sat out on her patio with toast and some of Esther's jam, Doreen had to wonder if Esther would know anything about Dennis or even his affairs in town.

Doreen hadn't checked in with Esther in a while, and the weeks just went by so fast that it was easy to see how time changed everything. She would drive over to see Esther, take the animals on a short walk in that area, and then from there drive farther downtown to meet Adelaide.

With that decided, Doreen headed inside.

Chapter 13

DOREEN PACKED UP the animals and drove to Wendy's consignment shop but parked in the alleyway, marveling at the case that she'd solved from here. She let her animals out, as she exited her vehicle, and walked closer to Esther's yard. When she heard a sound in the backyard, she called out, "Esther, is that you?"

"Well, who else do you think it'll be?" snapped the older woman. And she opened the gate and stared at her. "Oh, it's you."

Doreen winced. "Hey. I was just stopping by to see how you were doing."

"Are you sure you're not after my jam?"

Doreen laughed. "It'll take me a while to get through the stash you gave me. So you don't have to worry about my coming after your jam."

"What's wrong with it then?" she asked suspiciously.

Surprised, Doreen shook her head. "Absolutely nothing is wrong with it," she declared. "Matter of fact it's absolutely wonderful, but I know how important it is to you. So rest assured, as delicious as it is, I'm not trying to get more off you."

"Well, it is delicious. Of course it is," Esther confirmed, yet she still frowned. "However, it almost makes it sound as if you don't like it."

"Oh my goodness, no," Doreen corrected. "I had it on toast this morning."

"Good. No peanut butter?"

"No, not today I didn't," she replied. "Didn't even think about it."

"That's the way it's supposed to be. That jam's much better than any peanut butter."

Doreen could only smile and nod. "Just checking up to make sure all's well in your corner."

Esther finally relented. "Well, that's nice of you."

"How are your magpies?"

"A pain, as always," she said with spirit, as she pointed up to where a really big one was. "He's quite the tormentor."

"He looks like a wonderful specimen," Doreen noted. "So big and healthy."

"Yeah, that he is, probably too big and too healthy. He's probably been eating off me all these years."

"Then you are a credit to Mother Nature for helping out her species," Doreen stated. "Lord knows we all need help sometimes."

At that, Esther looked over at her. "Are you doing any better?"

"I am," Doreen said, with a smile. "I should be okay for money right now, at least same as you, with Bernard's reward. And, of course, I did solve another mystery, so that's always a feel-good thing."

Esther nodded. "I heard about that, and it was a good thing."

"You heard about it?" Doreen asked. At that, Esther just

gave her that knowing look. "Of course you did," Doreen replied. "Quite a bit of gossip surrounded that case, wasn't there?"

"I don't know. I don't listen to gossip," Esther replied, "but I did hear some of the rumors."

"That's good enough for me," Doreen said. "Anyway, have you had any more interruptions or garbage can incidences?"

Esther shook her head. "No, none. I don't get it. But, hey, as long as nobody's around to hassle me anymore, that's all good."

"Life's been quite peaceful then?"

"That was you, wasn't it?"

Doreen winced. "Well, to a certain extent it might have been me," she admitted, "but I can't really take the credit for all of it."

Esther *harrumphed*. "Well, at least those guys stopped doing it. I can't believe they were looking for that ring that had been up there the whole time."

"Would you have turned in the ring for that reward money?" Doreen asked, with a gentle smile.

Esther shook her head and shrugged. "I don't need any money, but thank you for sharing. Plus, if the magpies are happy, I'm happy."

That revealed so much about Esther that Doreen smiled. "I presume they're still happy up there."

"I don't think they even notice it is missing," Esther muttered. "I've been telling my ex over at the cemetery about it," she shared, "and my friends all thought it was quite a hoot." Doreen eyed her sideways, but Esther was staring off in the distance, before speaking again. "It's kind of fun to be involved in something like that."

"It can be fun, but it can also be kind of dangerous."

"You're supposed to learn to protect yourself, so you don't get hurt all the time," Esther scolded. "You might as well come in, while you're here anyway. I have some dog biscuits for this guy." Esther bent down to pet Mugs, who knew her soft spot and was already at her side, nuzzling her hand.

Doreen sighed. "He doesn't really need more."

"All dogs need more," Esther declared. "They need more of everything. More love, more hugs, more cuddles." She looked around and asked, "Where's the cat?"

"Oh, he's probably chasing your magpies," Doreen muttered in a quiet voice.

Esther spun, looking for the birds and the cat. "He won't hurt them, will he?"

She stared at Esther and then admitted, "Yes, he probably would, but hopefully we'll coerce him not to."

At that, Esther raced to the door and motioned for Doreen to follow her. "Come on inside. Get them all inside. I've got treats in here that he can eat. He doesn't have to go after my birds." As Esther made her way inside, she told Doreen in a scolding tone, "You should have him on the leash."

"I had him on a leash, but I was thinking that he didn't have to be on it today. I forgot about your magpies," Doreen noted apologetically.

Esther glared at her. "How can you forget my magpies?"

"I just wasn't thinking." And that was the honest truth. "I've been off my game a little bit these last few days," she shared in a tired tone. "It's this new case."

"What case is that?"

She quickly explained, and Esther nodded. "Right, that

would be a good one to solve. I never could understand how he could run away like that and leave his wife and kids. Everybody said he was a family man, but a family man doesn't do that to his sons and his wife."

"I agree with you there," Doreen replied. "Do you know much about it?"

"When you've lived here as long as I have, you get to know various people."

"Did you know him?"

"No, sure didn't," she said, "but the rumors were there. He always had affairs."

"Funny, that's something the wife didn't mention to me," Doreen replied in a dry tone.

Esther gave her a sharp look and cackled. "Why would she? She knew that you would find out anyway. If you ask me, last thing she wants is more mockery, which I'm sure she had more than plenty of back then."

"That's never a nice way to go through life, is it?" she murmured.

"You should know."

Doreen stared at her, but there didn't appear to be any ill will, just a natural comment about the reality of Doreen's situation. "I guess that's true," she agreed, then quickly changed the subject. "Do you have any theories on what happened to him?"

"Theories?" she repeated. "You're looking for theories now? Wow. You really must be lacking information."

Doreen winced at that accurate summation of her situation. "I am definitely lacking information," she confirmed. "So that's a very good point, but I keep hoping that something would break and that I'll find people who know something. I'm meeting a woman who had an affair with him a long time ago."

"Oh, that would be either Adelaide or … was it Elizabeth? I think there was also *hmmm* …" Esther pondered that. "I think there was a woman out in the Joe Rich area. She used to bring in the eggs. She told me one time that she made a really bad mistake with a married man, not realizing he was married."

"Do you think it's the same one?"

"I don't know. It was about the same time, though."

"What? Ten years ago?"

"Yeah, more actually," Esther added, pondering it. "I told her that she's got to stay away from men like that. She just mentioned something about she'd been a fool, but now she knew he was long gone."

"Good for her then," Doreen noted. "Not everybody takes that opportunity to get out of a situation."

"No, and that's even sadder," Esther said, "because you know they need to get the heck away from it."

"Sure, but, if it's been ongoing a long time, some women think that the guy will leave their spouse for them."

"More fool them," Esther said, with a cackle. "That's not the way it works."

"And yet maybe it should," Doreen suggested. "I mean, when you think about it, maybe if their affairs were made public, these men would stop doing it."

At that, Esther just studied Doreen and asked, "Do you really believe that?"

Doreen smiled and then shrugged. "No, I am sure they will just get trickier about finding ways to do it secretly."

"Exactly, and, although you can't blame just the women, you also have to accept that the women were probably missing a lot of signs because they wanted to believe him and didn't want to notice those signs. In this case though, the other woman was quite devastated because she hadn't believed that he was married, and it was quite a shock to her."

"That's never fun."

"No."

Esther made tea and sat down with Doreen. Esther lifted her leg to put it on the side chair.

"How are the ankles?" Doreen asked.

"Rough," she replied, glumly staring down at her legs. "Sometimes I keep thinking I should go into a home, where it'll be easier."

Doreen nodded. "If you're ready for that, it would be a lot easier on you. You'll get your meals and laundry and nursing care, if needed."

"If I don't need it, they will still give it to me. You know I can't stand to have things forced on me."

"I don't think they would force anything on you," Doreen noted, "but, if you needed extra help, you know that's what these places are for."

"I'm not quite there yet."

"At least you're hoping you're not there yet."

"I'm not there yet," she repeated firmly. "That time might come, but it's not here now."

"Good enough," Doreen said, with a cheerful smile. When the tea was done, she looked over to see Mugs, still being fed biscuits. "Good thing we're having a long walk today, Mugs. It'll take a while for you to wear off all those treats."

Esther smiled. "Oh, he's doing just fine. I keep forgetting how much I miss dogs, and then you come along and remind me."

"Having a pet is a heck of a responsibility, but they give so much joy back in life," Doreen shared. "I can't imagine what my life would be like without them now." As she got up, she asked, "I don't suppose you know how to get a hold of this woman in Joe Rich, do you?"

Esther shrugged. "I know which property is hers. It's the second right-hand turn, once you're on the highway past the sign. It's got a big, long gravel road."

"Does she have a husband?"

Esther pondered that. "I don't know if she does or not, so, if you'll go up there and talk to her, you may want to ensure your conversation is private."

Doreen accepted the warning in good grace because Esther was right. The last thing Doreen wanted was to get involved in an irate argument with a spouse or with somebody who didn't know about the affair. With a smile and a thank-you for the tea, Doreen went to take her leave, when Esther held out something in her hand.

"You might as well take this," she muttered, as she held out a jar of jam.

Doreen frowned at her. "I don't want to take all your jam," she protested.

"Good, because I won't give it all to you." And she glared at her. "But you can have this one." It was obvious that the gesture was coming from the heart, and Doreen didn't want to say anything to upset Esther, so Doreen smiled broadly. "You are, indeed, a very generous person."

Esther snorted. "Don't you pass that around," she snapped. "I have a reputation to uphold." And, with that, she went inside and slammed the door. But Doreen was no longer daunted by a slammed door. She knew that it hid a very gentle soul inside, and this was just Esther's way.

With a smile on her face, Doreen pocketed the jam and headed back to her car. There she put it in the glove box, so she wouldn't forget it, and slowly headed down toward the park, where she would meet up with Adelaide Bonner.

Doreen was a half hour early but had the animals on their leashes again and walked them around the park. She circled around and was almost right on time.

She sat down on the bench closest to the street but still in the park itself, where she could watch people coming and going. Seemed like everybody was outside enjoying the park, when another woman walked over to Doreen and stopped. Doreen looked up and then smiled. "Hey."

Adelaide nodded. "Obviously you're Doreen."

Doreen looked at the animals and nodded. "I guess I don't really need a calling card, do I?"

"No, they're quite an announcement already."

At that, Doreen smiled. "I won't be too upset about that." She chuckled. "They're all part of my family, so …"

Adelaide nodded and asked, "Do you mind if I sit?"

"Please do," Doreen replied.

As Adelaide sat down, she whispered, "I really don't like talking about this."

"I understand, but, until the mystery is solved, unfortunately it just keeps coming around and around."

"Which is why I'm here. I want you to solve this, and I want you to solve it for good, so I don't have to keep doing this."

"I would love to," she agreed, nodding in understanding. "It's not always quite so easy."

"I know, and I also know that Millicent trusts you," she shared. "So I'll do the same, and I'll trust you, … but I really would hope that I don't have to deal with this in public."

Doreen thought about it for a long moment. "I can't promise to keep you out of it," she shared, "depending on what you tell me, and I certainly can't promise that the police won't talk to you about any of it. However, I would very much hope that you don't need to be involved past this."

Adelaide hesitated and then admitted, "I guess I don't really have much choice, do I?"

"You do. Absolutely you do," Doreen stated. "And I really appreciate that you have come this far because, if people don't start talking, we'll never get answers."

"I thought everybody already talked lots back then," Adelaide quipped. "I stayed silent because my relationship with him was over and had been for a while. Yet, at the same time, it felt off. It felt strange, you know?"

"In what way?"

"Because I still cared, and I didn't realize at the time that he was married, but shame on me," she admitted, still with old bitterness tinging her voice. "I didn't break it off when I found out either."

"Ah." Doreen nodded. "That's two different things, isn't it? One to find out and another to take care of the matter once you do find out."

"And it's just not that easy, when you have all these other emotions involved. So, you keep trying to justify it, like, … *He's not happily married, and he'll leave his wife.* He said he was … I mean, he told me that he was … Many, many times he repeated that, but, of course, he didn't." She looked down at the animals again and asked, "Do you take them everywhere?"

"Not everywhere," Doreen replied, noting Adelaide was emotional and disturbed by all this and just needed to change the conversation, "but to a lot of the places, yes."

"Amazing," she murmured. "I've never really had that much to do with cats."

"They're definitely different from dogs," Doreen noted, "and they take a certain amount of work, but they also give me back way more in love."

"I've heard that before from various people," Adelaide shared. "I also think you're blessed to have them."

Doreen smiled at her. "I agree with that too."

Adelaide chuckled. "Anyway, I'm not sure what it is you expect me to say. I don't really have much else to tell."

"Maybe you can tell me, when you broke it off, what was his reaction when you did so?"

She pondered that. "Honestly, I think that was part of the reason why I didn't say anything. I broke it off finally, and he didn't seem to be too bothered, and that, … in its own way, really upset me."

"Of course," Doreen agreed, "because it just made you feel that the relationship was nothing to him."

"Oh, I don't think it was anything to him, whereas, to me, it had been a lot. I had recently buried a partner," she explained. "I was looking for that same love that I had back then, and, when Dennis said he was leaving his wife, and he was just figuring out how to settle up the farm and everything else, I was … That isn't a complicated process, but it became … I thought it was going somewhere, but then it became quickly evident that he wasn't leaving his wife, and he wasn't settling up the farm, and, indeed, I'm not even sure it was his farm either. So getting rid of it was out of the question."

"I understand that it is still quite complicated with the emotions involved alone," Doreen murmured.

Adelaide Bonner nodded. "It was."

"Do you have any idea why somebody would kill him?"

Adelaide looked over at Doreen, with a mild look of surprise. "After what I went through, I don't think it will be very hard to find people who wanted to or had the motivation to kill him," she shared, "but following through? Now that's a different story."

"Good point," Doreen acknowledged. "So do you think other women were in his life?"

"I know there were," Adelaide stated. "That's when I finally broke it off. When I realized that I wasn't the only one, and he was just stringing me along. Still, it was so difficult. I was hurt at the time, but I very quickly realized it was a fast escape for me. I could have been trapped in there for years, like some other people I know of."

Doreen nodded. "I have heard a few names mentioned."

"I know, and believe me. It was hard to deal with. When you hear the other names and realize that it's a long list, and you're just one of many?"

"I'm sorry," Doreen whispered.

Adelaide Bonner gave a headshake. "It's okay now. It really is. If nothing else it helps to show me that I've come a long way and that I'm not the same person I was back then." She smiled then. "It does help that I've already found another partner, and I'm quite happy right now. It's another reason I would like to ensure that nothing comes of this, that nothing comes out because I don't want him involved."

"Did he know you back then?"

"Sure," she replied, with a smile. "We were neighbors, but we certainly weren't sweet on each other. That's something that has grown over time."

"That may be a nice way to have a relationship," Doreen

noted, "as friends before lovers."

"Well, the lovers' part before friends certainly didn't work out long-term," she muttered, "so I was not against trying this way. Now I'm quite happily married, and I really would like to not have any of this brought up. He's a good man, and it would hurt him."

"Yes, but he's also an adult," Doreen stated, "and it was before his time. I don't think any of that would matter to him at this point."

"Maybe." She hesitated and then added, "Honestly I'm ashamed, and I would just as soon that nobody found out, especially him, but nobody hearing of this would be nice." She sat for a long moment.

"Where did you meet?"

"What do you mean? Like originally? I don't know. I think I was up at the farm at one point."

"No, like where did you go for your meetings?"

Adelaide winced. "My place most of the time," she shared. "I was alone. I had a place, so I guess—from his point of view—that was an easy answer." She shuddered. "It just goes to prove how much of an imbecile I was."

"Which isn't an issue now," Doreen clarified. "We're just looking to see where he could have been and what he might have been up to that somebody would have done something to him."

"For the longest time I entertained the thought that things had just gotten too hard for him, and maybe he just left. I mean, him and his wife? … As far as I know, those two used to have quite the fights, but I only found that out afterward, when I realized that they were still together. He didn't tell me that they were together. He kept telling me that he would leave her, and, of course, that's the same old story that so many of the guys say, isn't it?"

"Lots of times," Doreen admitted, moving cautiously. "Yet that doesn't mean that a woman, looking for love and pretty sure that it's here in front of her, won't listen to everything that she can listen to, in order to keep perpetrating the same myth."

Adelaide stared at her. "It almost sounds like you do understand."

Doreen gave her the gentlest of smiles. "Believe me. I am not without blame," she began, trying to be as gentle as possible, "and I have my own crosses to bear when it comes to relationships, but it's much easier to realize dysfunction once you have seen it yourself."

Adelaide nodded. "The good news is, the relationship I'm currently in is lovely. He's lovely, and, for that, I am so thankful. We're very happy," she shared thoughtfully, "and, yes, we would weather this. I mean, he might be upset and disappointed, but not more than I am at my own behavior. So I guess I'm not too bothered. I would just like to not have any of it come up again, if possible."

"With any luck," Doreen replied, "we could potentially solve this, and it can go down in history forever. A case closed. As long as it remains open, however, that's a different story."

Adelaide sighed. "Yeah, we went to my place. We used cell phones. We texted back and forth. I wasn't allowed to go up to the farm anymore because he had a lot of people working there, and it was still something he was trying to get loose from his wife. Of course I worked downtown, so Meredith and I didn't cross each other's space. In fact, that was the same with him too. In public, we didn't face off very often, but, when we did, we tried to ignore each other," she said. "Yeah, that was even more of an indication that we were doing something wrong. I just didn't want to believe it at the time."

"I understand."

"It was naughty, you know? It was fun. It was terribly exciting," she explained, "until it came to an end, and then it was just very odd, sad, and heartbreaking." She stood up and announced, "I have to get back to work."

"Okay." Doreen handed her a card. "If you think of anything, anybody who might have hated him in particular, anybody who might have had anything against him more than what we're talking about right now, any names that I can go look at or talk to, I would appreciate it."

Adelaide slowly nodded. "It just feels like tattling."

"Still, that doesn't solve his wife's problem with the farm or give his children answers."

Adelaide paled. "Oh, Lord, his children." She shook her head. "That was the hardest thing for me. I was shaken when I realized what I was doing to that family. … I just couldn't deal with it."

"Now you don't have to. Remember that," Doreen pointed out. "Other things are going on here, and maybe he just took off. Maybe he was done and just wanted to have a life on his own."

She shook her head. "I don't think so. I think he was murdered."

Doreen looked at her. "Well, that's two of you who feel that way."

"Two of his exes?" At that Doreen smiled, and Adelaide winced. "Never mind. I don't want to know who she was although I could guess considering one was supposed to be just a *good* friend."

"Good, because like you, she's more afraid about people finding out, about her being embarrassed, and about having to live with knowing what she did."

"It's a terrible thing to know that you've done something so wrong and to know you have no recourse to fix it."

"The only recourse you have is to do what's right, beginning now. Whatever that looks like may not be in the form that you think it'll take," Doreen explained. "Justice is justice, and it doesn't always come in a neat, tidy package. Sometimes it's messy. Sometimes it's ugly. And sometimes your sympathy is more with the attacker than it is with the victim. That's the thing about justice. It still matters though because that's the rules we live by, and, if somebody did kill him, even though they may have been fully justified in their minds and in other people's minds," Doreen said, with a pointed look, "it doesn't mean that it was the right thing for those kids."

"His kids need closure, but so do I. It was such a terrible time back then, and now that I've sorted my life and am so much happier, it's really hard to consider opening it all back up again."

"By your own words, you were just foolish. You believed because you wanted to believe," Doreen said. "Don't make it into something bigger than that."

Adelaide considered Doreen and then gave her a sad smile. "It's not quite that easy, you know?"

"Of course it isn't." Doreen chuckled. "Nothing is ever that easy. But we don't have to make it any more complicated than it is either. You had an affair with a married man. That's it. He is not around anymore, so be done with it. It's over. You broke it off. Maybe not as quickly as you wanted to, as you look back, and maybe not the right thing to have started in the first place, but it's over. You can't change it. The man has now been missing well over ten years, and I think it's time that it was solved. It's time for the kids to have answers, and it's time for his memory to be laid to rest."

Silence came from Adelaide.

"And for you," Doreen added, with the gentlest of smiles, "to stop hiding."

Adelaide looked at Doreen, and then a beaming smile broke out. "That," she replied, "makes a whole lot of sense." On impulse, she gave Doreen a huge hug. "Thank you for that. I hadn't really considered it in that light, but you're right. It is definitely way past time."

Doreen smiled.

Chapter 14

AFTER ADELAIDE RETURNED to her office, Doreen found herself wandering around City Park, taking in the sights. She loved the view and the marina; just the smell was inviting. She was enjoying the various gardens. She avoided going up to the big pavilion, where the wisteria grew, as that recently solved case was a little too close to her heart right now.

Still, an awful lot could be said about the people she was meeting on this case, and the people were still dealing with the pain of their own actions. It always amazed Doreen that we could tear ourselves apart on behavior that, in so many ways, really wasn't the worst thing that we could have done. However, in our minds it became the worst thing because it was something to be ashamed of. And, for these two women—Adelaide and Lilly Anne?—that seemed to be quite true.

Dennis obviously hadn't felt the same. He hadn't seemed to be plagued with guilt, even though he had had several relationships, several women hanging about in his life, all quite happily enjoying a relationship with him while he was married to Meredith, who was working the family farm the whole time.

Doreen knew that she would have to go talk to Meredith Polanski again, but Doreen dreaded it, as she would have to bring up some of these relationships, some of his betrayals. Doreen didn't see how his wife could not know about these affairs. Still, if Doreen had to be the one to tell Meredith, it would not be easy either. And, even if Meredith did know, she wouldn't want Doreen bringing it up. So Doreen needed answers, before she tore Meredith's life to bits and pieces again.

She walked through the park down below the large Spirit of Sail monument, picked up a coffee, and just enjoyed a little bit of time by the water. She strolled with the animals. Several people stopped to talk to her, commenting on Thaddeus especially, and Goliath on a leash. When she finally headed back to her vehicle, she heard a shout behind her. She turned to see a middle-aged man, racing toward her, literally running flat-out. She stopped, astonished. She certainly didn't recognize him. She looked around, wondering if he was calling out to somebody else, but he stopped in front of her, glaring.

"*You*," he snapped, "you need to stop this."

"Stop what?" she asked, eyeing him closely.

"Asking questions."

"That'll be a little hard to do," she replied ruefully. "I'm investigating a case, and I am sure that has nothing to do with you."

He shook his head. "No, no, no, no. You can't go around asking all these women... these questions. It's upsetting people."

She stared at him. "Maybe, but questions must be asked to get the answers we need."

He snorted at that. "You didn't need to talk to her," he

declared. "Now she'll be upset all day. I don't like it when she's upset," he snapped.

"What's your name again?" Doreen asked curiously. "Who is it that you think I was just talking to?"

He glared. "I don't just *think*," he stated, "I know. She told me that she was meeting you for lunch today, and I had absolutely no idea who you were, until I started doing some research. Once I figured out who you were, there was only one possible reason that you could want to speak to my wife, and that would be that louse that she had an affair with."

Doreen stared at him. "Okay, so you're Adelaide's husband, I presume. She told you that she was meeting somebody today, but she didn't tell you what it was about?"

He nodded. "That's not the reason I'm here, but because now she'll just worry."

Doreen chuckled. "That may be," she admitted, "but all you have to do is tell her that you know all about it and that it doesn't matter to you, and then she doesn't have to worry."

He continued to glare. "I want you to stop. I don't want you to talk to her anymore."

Doreen raised an eyebrow. "If I need to talk to her, I will," she stated succinctly. "And now that I know that you know, did you know Dennis at the time that he disappeared?"

"Yeah, he was an idiot. All he cared about was getting into the next woman's pants," he stated. "You always have one guy like that in town, and that was Dennis. He didn't care about his kids finding out. He didn't care about his wife finding out. He didn't care about nothing."

She stared at him, sensing the disgust in his voice. "Okay, and did you get angry at him because of the affair with your current wife, who wasn't your wife at the time?"

"No, of course not," he replied, with a shrug. "There wasn't anything to be angry about, except that I thought he was pretty despicable. He was hurting all these women, especially his wife and his kids. A couple times I told him that he should just take off and make life easier on everybody, but he would just give me the finger and carry on."

"Of course," Doreen noted. "He wouldn't listen to that kind of talk, would he? He was having too much fun."

"That's it exactly," he admitted in disgust. "I don't want you having anything more to do with my wife. She needs to let it go."

"Ah, you mean because you say so?"

He glared at her. "I don't want her hurt."

"Well then, clear up the air between the two of you, and it won't matter. Now if you'll excuse me," She turned, then looked back at him. "Outside of your having a motive for wanting Dennis to disappear, who else hated him?"

His jaw dropped. "I didn't kill him," he cried out. "See? That's the problem with people like you. You don't think about what you're saying. You just let anything fly out of your mouth, and it doesn't really matter anymore. You could potentially destroy someone with that mouth of yours."

"That's not quite true," she argued. "I do care, but I am looking to see who might have had ill will toward Dennis."

"Then my guess is that includes half the town," he snapped. "This guy was a major player, and he slept around with so many women. If you had a wife, she wasn't safe."

"Which, of course, is not giving credit or blame where it is due," she noted. Before he could interrupt again, she added, "These *wives* were not necessarily innocent. However, in both possible cases that I know of, the women were single.

They both knew he was married though."

"Right." He raised both hands. "That was a slip of the tongue. She wasn't my wife at the time."

"But obviously you feel very strongly about this."

"Of course I do. … The man's despicable." Then he stopped. "You should be talking to Rodney."

"Who's Rodney?"

"He is the guy who went to jail for attacking him."

At that, her jaw opened. "How come I haven't heard anything about him yet?"

"Most people have probably forgotten about him. He went to jail for attacking Dennis, about a year before he disappeared."

"What was the fight about?"

The guy gave her a look. "Rodney's wife. What else do you think?"

"What happened?"

"He went to jail for about six months," he replied, trying to jog his memory, "and then he got released somewhere around a few months before Dennis disappeared," he shared, with relish. "That's probably who did it."

"And yet, if that were the case, I'm sure the cops would have been hunting him down back then."

"Sure, but I don't think they could break his alibi." He shrugged. "Yet alibis are easily set up."

"If you say so."

He just gave a wave of his hands. "Of course they are, and that would have been the easiest answer."

"Doesn't mean easy is correct," she muttered.

"No, but it also doesn't mean that getting complicated about this is the way to go about it either," he snapped. "You go talk to him."

"Where is he?" she asked.

"He's up in the Joe Rich area. He's one of our neighbors, but he's kind of cranky, so we keep away from him."

"I wonder why," she muttered. "What about his wife?"

"They divorced, and she took off, went down to the coast I think. For all I know, he could have murdered her too." He started to laugh.

"Glad you think murder's a laughing business," Doreen replied stiffly, glaring at him.

He shrugged. "It's not my fault that these people are all such fools, but you stay away from my wife. She's a good woman, and she doesn't need your grief." And, with that, he stormed off again.

Chapter 15

DOREEN DROVE HOME slowly, her mind full, as she contemplated everything that she'd just learned. Rodney was yet another name that nobody had mentioned, whether it was just hindsight or everybody had forgotten about his involvement, or he had been a suspect back then and had been cleared, so his name didn't come up. Yet it still should have been in the files.

She would have to mention that to Mack. Maybe Rodney's name and any related investigation had been taken out of the file, when his alibi appeared to be good back then. Doreen would have to find out.

She pondered that as she drove home, and only after she was out of downtown and heading down Lakeshore Road did she notice a black truck had been behind her the whole time. Not that Kelowna's a big town. Not a ton of different areas to go around here. Therefore, if he wanted to run errands, there were only a few different street options. So Doreen and someone in a big black truck heading in this same direction was hardly news.

On instinct, she took a detour into a small parking lot, which contained a lovely little bakery and a grocery store.

She stepped out, with the animals still in the vehicle, and walked to the bakery, where she just waited. Sure enough the truck pulled in. The driver drove past her vehicle slowly, went to the far side, and just parked.

Frowning at that, she returned to her vehicle and turned it on and pulled out in the opposite direction. Hopefully she lost him then, if he was after her. She made it home without any further thought of that, driving her car into the garage.

Exiting, she turned to look around, still worried that somebody had followed her. However, not seeing anybody, feeling somewhat relieved, she closed the garage door and headed inside with the animals. As she unlocked the inner door, the animals raced in, as if they hadn't been home in days, making her smile at their antics. She was still trying to close the door, as Goliath decided at the last minute that he should go back out, when her phone rang.

She got twisted up on the cat's leash and fell down on her butt. She glared at Goliath, who sauntered past, as if for all the world he had nothing to worry about. When she finally answered her phone, she was breathless.

Mack asked, "What's wrong?"

She glared at the phone. "Why is everything always *wrong* to you?"

He snorted. "Because, with you, it's usually so."

"Nothing is wrong," she relented, with a sigh. "I was just trying to get in the stupid door, and Goliath tripped me up."

He gave a chuckle of laughter. "So now it's Goliath's fault?"

"Yes, it's Goliath's fault," she snapped. Then she sighed. "So do you have a reason for calling, or can I get up off my butt, take off my shoes and my coat, and put on the teakettle?"

"You can call me back in a few minutes if you want," he murmured.

"No, I'm fine." She quickly made her way to her feet, dusted off her pants, shut the door with a resounding *click,* and added, "Now I'm in at least, and I can go put on the teakettle."

"Where were you?"

"Downtown. I was talking to one of Dennis's former lovers."

"Interesting. Find out anything?"

"Lots of people hated Dennis," she replied, with a laugh.

"Yeah, that tends to be the way with guys like that, but anything concrete?"

"No, not yet, except apparently somebody did time for attacking him though."

There was a moment of silence. "I think I remember something about that. The lead detective on the case did talk to him at the time, but he had a sure alibi."

"Well, the husband of one of the wives caught me in the park today," and she quickly explained what he had to say.

"Wow, sneaking around on his wife at work? That doesn't sound like a great marriage either."

"No, I was thinking that myself," she murmured. "Anyway he was pretty happy to put me on this guy's trail. He was beyond upset too."

"Of course. Anything to keep you away from his wife."

"Oh, it's not as if I was thinking she was involved, but nothing like having somebody act like him to make you suspicious."

"I hear you there. Anyway, I thought I would pop by."

"Well, if you're popping by, why are we talking on the phone?" she asked in exasperation.

He laughed. "I wondered if you had picked a soup yet."

"Oh, gosh, I picked several of them, and then I keep changing my mind."

"Pick one, and then we'll do another one later," he suggested. "Do you have any onions at home?"

"Sure, you brought a bag last time."

"How about we make some French onion soup?"

She had visions of these fancy little bowls of onion soup covered in a great big slab of French bread and a lovely crust of Gruyere cheese on top of all that. "Can you make something like that?" she asked.

"We can try. I may not have French bread, or I may have a version of French bread but not quite what you're used to, plus a sharp cheese from my fridge," he replied, "but it'll all still make for a really good soup."

"I'm game if you are," she replied.

"Okay, and it doesn't take all that long to make. I'll start it when I get there."

When he ended the call, she put down her phone, happy to hear the teakettle whistling. She made herself a pot of tea and brought out the onions. She wasn't sure what all else she would need, but, wow, if she could get a bowl of French onion soup tonight, she would be one happy camper.

Particularly when her husband used to take the top off her soup all the time because it would make her fat. She thought back to all the little things that he used to do and winced. "You've got no business judging any wife," she murmured to herself. "Not when you were the poster child for being an idiot yourself."

Pouring a cup of tea, she moved out to the deck; it was almost time for Mack to show up. And just then she heard the truck pulling in. At least she thought so. … Only Mugs started barking, which wasn't his usual behavior when it was Mack.

She went to the front door, opened it to find the black truck that she'd seen in the mall, the one she had thought was following her, now driving into the cul-de-sac.

Mack had a black truck too, but it sure as heck wasn't like this one. This one was an old beat-up model, and, by now, that definitely looked suspicious. As it drove around, it completely ignored her, Yet, as she came to realize, standing here like an idiot was a guaranteed way to make it obvious where she lived. She quickly jumped back inside and slammed the door shut. Although she was afraid it was too late now. The guy had already seen her.

Chapter 16

Doreen greeted Mack on the front step a few minutes later. He hopped out, flashed her a big grin, which fell off his face. She stood there, with her back to the screen door, her arms across her chest, her feet wide apart, and she gave him a good frown.

His eyebrows shot up. "I'm not late," he began. "I'm a little early, so I'm not exactly sure why you're upset."

She sighed. "It's not about you."

He snorted. "Sure looks like it's about me."

She raised both her hands. "I'm upset in advance," she announced. He stared at her, then his lips quirked. That, for some reason, made her even more upset. "Because you'll get upset with me." At that, he stiffened and glared at her. She nodded. "See? You're already prepping for it."

He pinched the bridge of his nose and muttered, "You would make anybody crazy."

She snorted at that. "Looks like we're a matched set then."

At that, he looked up at her and, with a determined expression, raced up the last few steps, picked her up into his arms, and gave her a whopping kiss. "Finally you have come to the same conclusion I have."

She stared up at him, her brain still rattling from the kiss, and then tried to step back. When he wasn't having anything to do with it, she wiggled and wiggled. "That is having the opposite reaction to what you want," he murmured in a smoky voice.

She gasped and said, "That's not fair."

He laughed and released her. "Maybe not, but doesn't change the fact that you finally stated that we were a matched set."

"Of course we are," she replied, "because you could drive anybody batty."

At that, he laughed. He opened the door, ushered her inside, and said, "Come on. You can tell me what's going on inside."

"Why?" she asked, feeling suddenly contrary.

"Because right now you're drawing a crowd."

She turned to look around, but only birds were there. He nodded behind her, and she spun to see Richard, standing on his front porch, his arms over his chest, and a big smirk on his face.

She glared at him. "You have no reason to laugh."

"Maybe not, but you do give me a reason to smile."

At that, she wanted to race over and smack him one, but Mack held her firmly in place. She sighed. "Well, I'm glad you got your entertainment for the day."

He nodded. "You're right. It is very entertaining watching the two of you. Can't wait until you get married. Then things should calm down." With an eye roll at that, Richard just walked back into his own house calmly, as if he hadn't just dropped a bombshell.

She turned ever-so-slightly and stared up at Mack. "You

know I'm still trying to get a divorce, right?" she asked, her tone ominous.

He grinned at her and nodded. "How could I forget? He's been such a *wonderful* addition to our world."

At that, her shoulders sagged. "I'm being slow about it, I guess."

"Sometimes you are, yes," he agreed.

And a little too fast for her liking. She glared at him again.

He held up his hands. "I suggest we call it a truce right now," he said. "Let's head inside, and you can tell me what's got you all riled up."

"Don't you already know?" she asked suspiciously.

He sighed. "You haven't told me, so how could I know?"

"I figured that, seeing how you always seem to know when I'm in trouble, you already have the advanced warning on this one."

He stopped, looked at her carefully, and asked, "What kind of trouble are you in?"

"Come inside," she muttered, slamming the door behind them. "I don't need the neighbors to have any more entertainment over this."

He wisely didn't say anything to that, as she walked inside and sat down on the living room chair. "You better take a seat. Before I'm done, you'll be roaring at me anyway."

He slowly sagged into the other chair. "Okay, now you really need to tell me what is going on." She slowly explained, at least as much as she could.

"I knew about everything already, so what's different?" And he was truly puzzled by it.

"Just before I got home, on the way home, what I didn't tell you was I thought … I was being followed." His brows came together in a dark frown. She nodded. "Of course I had no real way of knowing, and then I heard a truck coming up into the cul-de-sac just a few minutes ago, and I thought it was you."

He stared at her, and, with a knowing look, said in a grim tone, "Carry on."

"I stepped out to see if it was you."

"Of course it wasn't me, and not only wasn't it me," he stated, his voice becoming thick with anger, "this person in the truck *saw* you?"

She nodded slowly. "Yeah, exactly."

He slowly sagged into the chair, his mind obviously buzzing. Finally he shared in a grim voice what she hadn't mentioned yet. "So you're saying that, *if* you were followed, *if* this truck driver cared about who you were, then now he knows where you live?"

She nodded glumly. "Yeah, that's about it."

"*Great.* How is it you always manage to get into these situations?"

She opened her mouth to refute it and then shrugged. "I don't know, just lucky I guess."

At that, he burst out laughing.

She smiled and asked, "So we're good?"

"No, we're not good," he declared, with a hard glance in her direction. "We're a long way away from good, but we're getting there."

She beamed. "See? I always liked that about you. You get in, you get angry, and then you get back out again."

He shuddered. "I can't even imagine that this is getting in and getting out of anger," he clarified, "but obviously the conversation has to shift to concern about *whether* this person was following you and, if he *was* following you, *why?*"

"I was wondering that myself. It didn't seem to make a whole lot of sense."

"And yet you know as well as I do that things don't make sense until we get more answers."

"I was thinking that maybe you could help me get answers." He frowned at her. She shrugged. "Unless you think it's really nothing. In which case, then I'm happy to just ignore this whole thing."

He scrubbed his face. "I need to get my mind wrapped around this. First off, have you been looking at anything other than the Dennis Polanski case?"

She shook her head. "No, I haven't."

He nodded. "So you're thinking that you may have shaken something loose?"

"I don't know about loose or whether just my questions angered somebody."

"Which, in this case, is quite likely," Mack noted thoughtfully. "You do have a habit of pissing people off."

She glared at him and then her shoulders sagged. "I don't *try* to piss people off. You know that, right?"

He cracked a smile at her. "Whether you do that on purpose or not isn't the issue," he pointed out. "The fact of the matter is, it does seem to have that same result."

She wouldn't argue with him because what could she say? Chances were, he was right. "It does seem a little foolish though," she murmured.

"What does?"

"That anybody would be upset at what I'm doing."

"Why is that?" he asked curiously.

"Because Dennis has been gone a long time. Why would anybody be bothered about it now?"

"You already know the answer to that." Mack stared at

her. "It's entirely because now something has shaken loose. And, whether you like it or not, you're starting to get a heck of a name."

She nodded. "It's really hard to hide now too. Everybody recognizes me." When his lips quirked, she glared at him. "It might be funny for you, but it's not so much for me. Mack, I swear I've lost the element of surprise."

He smiled at her. "Yeah, that's what happens. You start to be a success at something, and people who don't want anything to do with you are afraid that you might have answers or solutions that they don't want you to find out."

"Then they shouldn't go off and do nasty things to people," she said. "I mean, how is that fair?"

He stood. "It's not fair. At the same time …"

She nodded and rose and walked into the kitchen to put on coffee. As she stood and stared out the window, she heard him muttering behind her. She looked back at him. "Do I really bring this on myself?"

He shook his head. "The work you're doing brings it on. You're not bringing it on deliberately." Then he stopped and added, "You don't do it for the thrills of danger."

She shook her head. "No, I do not," she agreed in a determined voice. "I was down at City Park, talking to Adelaide Bonner. Her mother was a friend of Millicent's, and Adelaide had had an affair with our missing man."

"Right. Apparently there were several of them."

She nodded and turned around. He was looking at something on his phone. "Are you even paying attention?"

He smiled. "I'm bringing up the case file on my phone."

"Ah." She shrugged. "Sorry, I'm still irked by this."

"With good reason," he replied cheerfully. "It seems like you've antagonized somebody again."

"And yet, what could they possibly want?"

He shrugged. "In a case like this, it could be anything," he replied, studying her closely. "If it's related to this case, and I'm saying *if* because obviously we don't know that."

She had to agree with that. "Fine," she muttered. "But then, if it's not, what would it be related to?"

He stared at her and sighed. "Over the last month or two or three or four, don't you think you have pissed off enough people that maybe somebody decided to find out where you live?"

"But why follow me?"

"That's the part that got me. *If* he was following you," he pointed out, looking at her for confirmation, "then that is a concern. Doreen, just because they know where you live doesn't mean that they'll follow through on any kind of threat."

"Maybe not, but they've already followed through on something."

"Exactly." He pondered the case notes on his phone. "We have noted that he had several affairs, but everything ended amicably. We also spoke with all known parties at the time, but, since Dennis was an adult, there was always the chance that he just got up and walked off. So it was listed as a missing person's case …" Mack lifted his head to face Doreen. "Unfortunately a lot of times we do have cases where people just get up and walk away."

"What does it take for something like that?" she asked, walking closer. "I mean, what kind of mindset does somebody have to be in to just throw it all away—wife, kids, farm, bank accounts, credit cards, love affairs, everything?"

"Well, on the surface, everything *appeared*," he replied, with emphasis, "normal and fine."

"So?"

"Under the surface though," he added, still looking at the case file on his phone, "all kinds of things can sit there and can churn about. For all you know, his marriage wasn't very good, and he was looking to get out. Maybe he did leave with a lover we hadn't found out about yet."

"The marriage was, indeed, no good. Adelaide told me that Dennis and Meredith fought like crazy. Did anybody else leave town at the same time?" she asked him.

"No way to know," he said. "We can't keep track of more than one hundred thousand residents of Kelowna."

She pondered that and then agreed. "I suppose, if people want to leave, they'll do everything they can to make sure that they do leave."

"And you also know that it's not that hard. They save up enough cash, then just pack up and decide that life is better somewhere else, and they go. Or maybe things got too hard for him here. Maybe he got in trouble with too many husbands—or too many women—or maybe he just decided, *Screw it*. He would just leave, start fresh somewhere."

She winced at that. "Somebody like that won't start fresh. They'll just cause chaos wherever they go."

"The thing is, … it's Dennis's chaos. You have to remember that he brought this all on himself."

"Oh, I agree," she murmured. "Definitely agree with that. It doesn't negate the fact that we have two young men now who are missing their father, and nobody has any answers."

"And, for that reason alone, I'm all for you looking and sorting out if you can come up with anything," Mack shared. "As you know, we don't have the man-hours. We did the investigation back then. Every once in a while things come up that we wonder about it, but, if there are no new avenues to pursue, not much that we can do. We have to stay on top of everything else that's happening, which is a lot."

She winced at that. "It *is* a lot," she noted. "I'm sorry I ever bothered you guys or ever judged you."

He chuckled. "Now if everybody in town would have that same epiphany, life would be a lot easier for us."

"Agreed." She sighed. "It's just frustrating when you think that somebody knows something."

"But it's always that way," he reiterated. "Somebody always knows something, even if they don't know that they know it, but answers are out there. Just not everybody is, one, willing to tell us, or, two, willing to even talk to us in any way that we can define if they have any information that they might know of."

"Sometimes, and that's quite possible in these older cold cases too," she added, "people pass on, and the information dies with them."

"And then in a case like this, we don't have any proof that he did leave on his own, but neither do we have any proof that there was foul play."

"It's always about proof, isn't it?" she muttered in disgust.

He chuckled. "And you would be the first one to get upset if we accused anybody without proof."

"I know. I know. I know." She raised both hands in frustration. The coffee finished dripping, and she poured him a cup and slumped down on the chair beside him.

"Why don't we go over what you found and see if a fresh set of eyes makes a difference," he suggested, "and, while we're doing that, I'll put on the soup."

Chapter 17

AT THE MENTION of *soup*, Doreen brightened immediately. "You're okay to make soup though?" she asked. "I don't know that this is an easy one or a hard one."

He shrugged. "The version I make isn't hard, and it's certainly tasty. I'm just warning you that it may not taste the same as your version did."

"I haven't had it for a long time. I just know I really enjoyed it."

"Good enough," he replied cheerfully. "Then I'll take a chance, and we will make my version." And, with that, he bounded to his feet, started with water in the big stock pot, as she hovered beside him.

"What's that for?" she asked.

He looked over at her and replied, "Broth."

"Right." Then she frowned. "Don't you need onions for broth?" He pointed out the bag that she had left on the counter. "Okay, I'll be quiet, and I'll just watch."

At that, he burst out laughing. "It's your insatiable curiosity that's helped you to solve these problems," he noted. "You get a hold of something, and you just won't let go."

"Yeah, that would be somewhere along a bulldog type of

attitude," she muttered.

"Nothing wrong with that." He laughed at her growing irritation. "You could still go into law enforcement."

"No, I can't, but I appreciate the vote of confidence."

He looked over at her and said, "I hate to see you despondent."

"I'm not so much despondent as just frustrated because it seems that everybody hides secrets. If they would just be open and honest, the rest of this wouldn't be necessary."

He chuckled. "Wouldn't be necessary absolutely, but, considering a lot of these people hide all this information because they've done something wrong, then it helps to understand what they're up to."

"Sure, but everybody's up to something. That's the bottom line here. Everybody I meet has some kind of a secret somewhere in their past."

"Even you," he said, turning to look at her, his grin flashing.

"I suppose. I mean, I wouldn't want everybody to understand what my marriage was like," she shared.

His smile fell away, and he nodded. "No, and you're right. That is a secret that you are entitled to keep, and, of course, other people, if they knew, would be quite open about making sure the rest of the world knew."

"Exactly, but I won't kill somebody to keep it quiet."

"No, and that's a good thing," he replied, with a laugh. "You're right. I think everybody has secrets. Everybody has things that they have done that maybe they wish they hadn't done or at least wish they could have had a chance to do in a different way. However, that doesn't make them criminals."

"No, I get that," she agreed, watching him, as he worked efficiently as always in the kitchen. "You know that's one of the things about you in the kitchen that I really like." She came up behind him to study the growing pile of thinly sliced onions.

"What? I can cut onions without crying?"

She laughed. "No, just the fact that you can do it all so efficiently. It's not a stress or a big deal to you. You just pick up a knife and get started. You make everything look effortless."

He frowned. "I guess I can see how you would think that."

"That's another reason why. … You're good at it. You put things together and slice and dice. The next thing you know, a meal is there."

"That is something that you will get better at, as time goes on," he noted. She looked at him doubtfully. He smiled and added, "I promise."

"Okay, I'll hold you to it," she warned.

"Tell me what else you found out today." She went over Adelaide, the woman she met at the park. "And tell me again what her husband said."

She went back over that conversation, grabbing her notes, so she could remember it all, adding a few bits and pieces for clarity. "Again, nothing bad," she said, "but wouldn't it be nice if he hadn't done the cloak-and-dagger stuff just to talk to me?"

"Do you think he would tell Adelaide when he goes home tonight?"

"I told him to, but, as you know, I don't think people tend to listen to me."

He burst out laughing at that. "No, I don't imagine they do either," he muttered. "Most people don't take kindly to being told what to do."

"And yet"—she shook her head—"I know that's not my problem, even though I think the world would operate in a much better way if people wouldn't do things like that."

"Of course they won't listen to your advice, but …" He wagged his eyebrows at her. "A lot of people would have also said that you could have listened to your nan's advice many years ago too, and left Mathew sooner."

"You're right," she agreed. "Believe me. Lots of times lately I thought about it too. All the years that I wasted and didn't have her in my life because of him."

"And that's not what we're doing today," he stated firmly. "Mathew is on the way out of your life, and, with any luck, *is* out of your life, has finally signed *all* the paperwork, and we'll have a completely different scenario for you to smile about soon."

She chuckled. "I won't say no to that. I do think your scenario is way too simplistic, but I will be more than happy if it did turn out that way."

"Let's just put that out there, and hopefully it will come to pass," he said, with a smile. "Life isn't always a hardship."

"Since I've come here, it's been … *challenging*, I would say, mostly because I didn't know what I was doing or how I was supposed to be doing anything. However, it has been really good overall. It has been a hugely wonderful experience."

"Good," Mack said. "That is very important. Life's too short, as we keep reminding ourselves, and we need to make the most of everything."

"I get it," she said, suddenly yawning. "Oops, sorry about that," she added, wide-eyed. "Don't know where that came from."

"Well, you have had an awful lot of days, weeks, where

you've been under a lot of stress," he noted. "I wouldn't be at all surprised if you don't need weeks and weeks of sleep to catch up."

"Ah," she replied, "as soon as I have even a half-decent night, I'm already raring to go on the next thing."

"Which is another interesting aspect to you," he said. "I mean, not everybody is quite so eager and ready to dive into the next case."

"They fascinate me," she murmured. "People fascinate me—what they do, how they do it, why they do it," she shared. "All of it is interesting." He didn't say anything but continued to dice and chop. "Maybe it makes me a little too curious."

He laughed at that. "I don't know about a *little too curious*, but it definitely makes you one of those kinds of people who keeps an eye on everything and learns from it. That's the important part. You do learn from it."

"That's a good point too," she muttered.

"You don't really think about it, do you? Well, you need to because all this involves change. All this is different and unique. Sometimes it's easy, and sometimes it's not."

"So far it hasn't been easy at all," she admitted in astonishment, looking over at him.

He chuckled, and she watched as the onions were sautéed just enough to caramelize them, and then dropped into this big pot with the broth. The aroma of fresh sautéed onions filled the air. "Wow, I forgot just how much I love this kind of food."

He looked over at her. "Yet you haven't mentioned it before."

"As long as the weather was good," she explained, "I was totally okay with sandwiches and salads. Yet now that it's getting a little colder, you know I was just starting to think that maybe I needed to add other kinds of food."

"It's always a good idea to add in other foods, to eat a variety," he agreed, with a smile. "And there's absolutely no reason not to have something like this in summer too."

"I'm glad to hear that," she muttered, "because anything you can teach me is a help down the road too."

He nodded. "We'll keep working on it, a couple dishes at a time. Are you writing down notes?"

"No, but I should be, shouldn't I?" She sighed but got up. "That's another thing. It feels as if I write everything down now."

He burst out laughing. "Are you trying to say that you're getting old and don't like it or that your memory is going and that you're afraid you'll end up like Nan?"

"That would be something, wouldn't it?" Doreen gave a headshake. "None of those actually. I was just thinking that, even just now, as you mentioned that, asked if I was writing it down, that I should be writing down so much more. It's not so much that I forget it—well, I do forget some. That's part of it, but you also forget the nuances of how people say things and their eye movements and their facial expressions, just all of that," she shared. "It seems so easy at the time, how you'll always remember it. Then you walk away from those people, interviewing more people, and it's like, wow, what was it they did back there?"

He smiled. "Even learning that right now is huge. You should be writing it down. Write it all down so that, when you need it, you have it there to refer back to. Now let's go over those notes again on Dennis's cold case."

She stopped, looked at the soup pot. "How long do we have?"

"We have enough time to go over your notes," he stated firmly.

She smiled. "Even if we didn't, you would make sure, right?" she asked in a teasing voice.

"Maybe," he muttered. "I'll just let this simmer for a little bit."

Then she noted the loaf of French bread on the counter. "Did you bring that with you?" Surprised, he looked at her and nodded. "Wow." Her shoulders sagged. "I didn't even see you bring it. Can you just do regular toast with it?"

"You can do all kinds of things," he replied, with a smile. "Traditionally it's French bread on top of French onion soup," and he cut off big, thick slabs.

"Where did those bowls come from?" It just hit her, she'd never seen them before.

He chuckled. "You need to sit down and relax. I got them out of the cupboard in front of you."

"Oh, wow," she muttered. She sat here and watched, trying to put more effort into tracking and seeing what he was doing, and she realized that the cheese was going on top of the toast, as he ladled up the bowls and put the toast and the cheese on top, and then put them in the oven. She looked at him and asked, "What if I want seconds though?"

"Then we make up seconds. It's really not hard, and it's not a big deal."

"Are you sure?" she asked, frowning. "Because it looks like it could be a big deal."

"It's only a big deal if you make it a big deal."

She rolled her eyes at that. "Sometimes things seem to be a big deal, even when they aren't."

"And that's a good point, but it's really not an issue."

"Okay, good, because I might be hungry," she shared,

looking over at him.

"I suspect you would be hungry, particularly once you taste this."

"Oh, there we go," she teased. "Look at that ego."

He rolled his eyes. "Anything else in your notes?"

"Not enough to make a difference," she stated in disgust. "No threats, nothing. I do need to talk to the man who served time for beating up Dennis. *Rodney*."

"In other words you've done all the groundwork, and you still have nothing, right?"

"Yeah. How disgusting is that?"

He grinned. "Remember that part about police work is 90 percent footwork, 10 percent deductions?"

"I got the theory part down pat," she stated. "I do okay on the footwork, but it still really bugs me that most of the footwork is talking to people who don't want to tell the truth."

"If you were somebody who had done as much wrong as these people, and you didn't want to go to jail for the rest of your life, you would be pulling a stunt like that too."

"Yeah, well, in the first place, I would have stepped up and held up my hands and confessed. No way I wouldn't. People would take one look at my face, and they'd know the truth."

At that, he leaned over, kissed her gently, and murmured, "Don't change. Don't ever change." He propped open the kitchen door and asked, "Want to eat outside?"

"Absolutely." And then she looked at the oven. "Is it ready?"

Such astonishment filled her tone that he burst out laughing. "Absolutely, and, yes, there's lot of time to make another serving if we want it." She scampered out to the patio, rubbing her hands in delight, as she waited for him to bring out the hot bowls of soup.

As soon as they sat down outside, the smell of that beautiful French onion soup filled the air, and she sighed happily. "This is not what I expected today, but it's lovely." Then she dug right in.

Chapter 18

Wednesday, Wee Morning Hours...

DOREEN WOKE UP in the middle of the night, Mugs tense and growling beside her. She reached out a hand to calm him, noting the glowing wide eyes of Goliath and Thaddeus. If everybody was awake, something was seriously off. The question was, what was off? How badly off?

She slipped out of bed and over to the window and looked out. Everything in the backyard looked normal. Quiet and dark, no moving shadows. She headed downstairs to check out the front yard from the living room window. Somebody was walking in the cul-de-sac, not in her yard or anyone's yard, just wandering through the cul-de-sac, as if checking it out or at least clearing the area. No reason to be upset by it, as he wasn't doing anything, but his presence was odd. She couldn't find a reason to stay calm about it either. As things went, this was one of the ones that definitely didn't make her feel good.

She watched as he went from one door to the other but didn't open the door or knock, as if *casing the joint*. She frowned as he was too far away to take photos. Not to mention it was too dark out. Still it could be just somebody that was lost. Although this was not how somebody who was lost would act, at least not in her books.

As he got closer to her place, her muscles tensed. Mugs had jumped up, so his nose was sitting above the windowsill, but he still couldn't see out. She bent down and picked him up, and, as soon as he saw the other man, he started to bark.

The man froze, and rather than coming toward her and Richard's house, he turned and headed out of the cul-de-sac.

"That's why"—she kissed Mugs on his forehead—"we keep dogs." Of course there were a lot of reasons for keeping Mugs, but that was the biggest one for a lot of people. Dogs were a deterrent for anybody who was up to no good.

She waited and watched to see if the stranger came back, but, after ten minutes, there was no sign of him. Now he would have pinpointed probably where the house with the dog was, and, in that sense, she may have done herself in too. If he hadn't realized necessarily who was living where, that would have helped him to pinpoint her location, presuming he was looking for her.

What if he didn't know what she looked like? What if he didn't know anything about her except the vehicle? And that she had a dog? It's quite possible that he had only seen her from a distance and didn't know what she looked like, and now she'd given him yet another piece of the puzzle. Frowning at that, she checked her clock—only 2:30 in the morning. Definitely not a normal time for people to be out wandering around. She wasn't even sure what to do with that scenario but knew she would have to tell Mack about it, though she didn't want to ruin his sleep, and there was no need to call right now, as the man was gone.

Nothing had happened, and, for the rest of the night, she was pretty sure nothing would happen. Yet, as she went back to bed, she knew that *sleeping with one eye open* was foolish. Still, it's what she found herself doing, constantly waking up, listening, then drifting back under again, only to wake up and drift back under again. Didn't make for a very good night's sleep, that's for sure.

Chapter 19

WHEN DOREEN WOKE later that morning, she remained in bed for a long time, with the animals wrapped up around her, even Thaddeus was seated on her butt. She sighed and shifted. Thaddeus gave a squawk and walked up and over, as she rotated to her back. When he was finally on her ribs, where she could see him, she smiled at him. She gently stroked his feathers. "Good morning, buddy."

He squawked, "Good morning, buddy. Good morning, buddy."

She laughed. "That's a new one for you too, isn't it?"

"That's a new one for you too. That's a new one for you too."

She sighed. "Just means you're in fine form this morning."

Instead of responding to that though, he cried out, "Thaddeus is hungry. Thaddeus is hungry."

"Ah, well, if you're hungry, I bet the rest of the gang is too," she muttered. She looked over at the clock, and her eyebrows shot up. "Wow, it's almost 8:30." That was unusual for her. She got up, still groggy and unsettled, had a quick shower to try and stave off the rest of that horrible feeling, and headed downstairs. Dressed, but with wet hair, she hadn't even bothered putting it up. So the still-damp locks hung down her back. She put on coffee, knowing she would need it even more today. With that dripping, she headed outside to the patio. As she stood there, she heard Richard working in his backyard. She called out to him, "Richard, did you hear anybody last night?"

"Hear anybody how?" he muttered. He poked his head over the top of the fence and glared at her.

She nodded. "Somebody was walking up to each of our houses at about two o'clock in the morning last night. I don't know what he was up to."

He shook his head. "No, I didn't know or hear anybody. Most of us are asleep at that hour." He glared at her.

"Well, I was asleep, until this guy woke up Mugs."

At that, he stared down at the dog and then shrugged. "That's your fault."

She sighed. "Yes, thank you for that. I guess that just means that you didn't hear anybody."

"No, I didn't. I just told you that." And, with that, he dropped down behind his side of the fence again.

"He was coming to your house next," she called out.

His head instantly popped over the fence again. "What do you mean?" he asked suspiciously. She explained what she'd seen. He stared at her. "Rubbish. Nobody would come here. I have nothing for anybody to steal."

"Neither do I," she declared in astonishment. "I sold everything or gave it all away."

He laughed. "Good on you. I still don't have anything of any value though."

"Doesn't mean they know that," she pointed out. "For

all you know, he was just looking for the next house to case."

He continued to glare at her. "None of this would have happened if you hadn't moved in here."

As it was an old story, and she was too tired to even listen to it, she waved him away. "Go back to what you were doing, and keep in mind somebody could be slinking around." He disappeared to the other side, and she sighed.

"Why is it the coffee's never done?" she muttered, yet headed inside, knowing that it had to be ready now, surely. As she poured herself the biggest cup she had in the house, she took it outside and wrote a text message to Mack but then didn't send it, thinking that it was too long and too convoluted. Better off that she would tell him when he got over here tonight. If he came over tonight.

They'd had multiple bowls of soup last night, even though one was probably enough. However, she had been incredibly hungry. Of course Mack justified a single bowl of soup wouldn't do her a whole lot of good, but, after the second one, she'd been more than full. He even seemed to like it too, although he had doubled up on the cheese and the French bread topping his second bowl. If she hadn't been quite so full, she would have done the same. A bit of soup was left, and she smiled at that. Leftovers had become gold in her world.

It was a meal that she didn't have to make, a meal that was already prepped and ready, and she was just dying to get into it. Yet not for breakfast. She didn't think she could stomach a bowl of French onion soup for breakfast.

While she sat here, sipping her coffee, willing the world to give her a chance to wake up, Nan called. "Good morning."

"Oh, dear," Nan replied. "You don't sound very good."

"Rough night," she said, by way of an explanation, "but I'm fine."

"I'm glad you're fine. I still don't like that you're having all these rough nights though. You're too young for that."

She chuckled. "Oh, I'm glad to know that there is an age for one to be allowed to have bad nights," she muttered, "because, man, oh man, I'm not looking forward to that stage."

"You should come down here," Nan declared crossly. "It's probably all that worry about these cases."

"Maybe. I'm sipping my first cup of coffee right now, which I rather desperately need."

"Well, as soon as you're done with your coffee, come down," Nan repeated. "I'll find some treats for you." With that, Nan rang off.

Doreen wondered how long she could delay her visit, not because she didn't want to go see Nan, but she really wanted more coffee.

She got up and poured a second cup and sat down again. However, it bugged her because she had to leave. So she drank it as fast as she could, and then, with the animals in tow, she headed to Nan's. The walk itself was beautiful, but Doreen was apparently too tired and too ornery to even enjoy it.

Chapter 20

BY THE TIME Doreen got to Nan's, it seemed that the trip went way too fast and that the day had already started to the point that she had missed out on all that early morning wake-up time to just sit and rest and enjoy Mother Nature. Feeling slightly disgruntled and yet knowing she needed to let it go before she got to Nan's, otherwise Nan would be all over her with questions. Arriving at the patio, Nan was waiting for her.

"Well, you look better than I thought you would." Nan bent over to greet a very happy Mugs and even Goliath wove between her legs with affection.

Doreen winced. "That's nice. I gather you thought I would come looking pretty rough."

"After what you told me this morning"—Nan laughed—"that's to be expected." She reached out an arm for Thaddeus who immediately moved over to cuddle up against Nan's neck.

"Maybe, and it was a bad night, but a pot of coffee helped a lot."

"Cup or pot?"

"Pot," she admitted instantly, and then she laughed.

"Just a two-cup pot, but I'm still very much a coffee lover."

"There are worse things to be addicted to," Nan noted. "However, I hope you're not too full because I have put on the teakettle."

"Tea would be lovely." She wouldn't mind a treat or two either.

"And, even if it isn't what you want, you'll drink it because you're a good girl, right?"

Doreen smiled at her grandmother as she sat across from her gently stroking her old friend. "You know that I always love coming down and having tea with you. The animals do too."

Nan relaxed. "I do love to see you coming for tea. We haven't had tea for a couple days."

"Has it been that long?" Doreen asked in surprise. "Surely not?"

"Yes."

"Oh, sorry about that."

"That's all right. I've been busy too. So it's been fine. And I understand that you've got lots of things to keep flowing."

"Yeah, I sure do." Doreen stifled yet another yawn. Mugs, as if being of the same mind, slumped at her feet and started snoring.

Nan frowned at her. "You really didn't have a good night, did you?"

She shook her head, "No, I sure didn't, but that's okay. There are other days to have good nights."

But Nan kept a wary eye on her.

Doreen laughed. "It's okay. I won't explode or do anything silly."

"Well, that would be nice. I just want to confirm that

you won't do anything you wouldn't normally do because you're so tired."

"I don't think so. I'm not *that* tired."

Nan didn't look convinced. However, after she poured the tea, she added, "In regard to the case …"

Doreen stared at her. "What did you find out?" she asked, sitting up straighter.

"Nothing unfortunately. I was hoping you'd found something," Nan chuckled. "Still, is there anything you like better than a tidbit of information?"

"Yeah, a tidbit of information that means something."

Nan burst out laughing. "That's a fine distinction. We definitely want the kind of information that will make a difference, don't we?"

Doreen nodded. "That we do. Enough information is out there that already seems nefarious and not exactly clear. So anything that makes a difference would be lovely."

"How did your talk yesterday go?" Nan asked. "It's so hard not being able to share any information on this right now …"

"I know but it's important. And the meeting was fine, although I don't know about her husband."

Nan frowned. "What about him?"

"Oh." Doreen hesitated and realized that she'd probably already gone too far and couldn't back out now. And so Doreen told Nan about the man who'd run her down at the park.

"Good Lord, I've never met her husband, but I've heard that she's really happy."

"She might be happy, but he sure doesn't trust her."

"That's terrible." Nan shook her head.

"All he had to do was ask, and it would be much better

off for Adelaide's sake, if he did ask his wife or if she had volunteered the information," Doreen pointed out.

Nan winced. "Yes, I know you're quite right there. ... It would be much better if she did speak up and particularly before it became something else, other than a good thing."

At that, Doreen smiled. "The problem often is, she just doesn't want anybody to know."

"Of course not." Nan shuddered. "Who wants to have all your failures reported?"

"I don't know so much about it *being reported*," Doreen clarified, "but, when you think about it, an awful lot in life happens. Yet people are not being very honest about it, and they hide it. When they hide it, it makes things worse."

Nan chuckled. "It's all that relationship stuff, my dear."

Doreen raised her hands. "Maybe it's because I'm really tired today. Maybe it's because I'm frustrated that people are doing all this talking around stuff but not really saying what they knew, but it seems to me that Dennis had it all, and he had as many affairs as he wanted, and he had the farm, and he had a hardworking wife, and he had two sons. Dennis had everything."

"And?" Nan asked. "What's the punch line, dear?"

"There was no reason for him to just pull up stakes and take off," she replied, "unless he's been siphoning a pile of money and had it set aside or had a very wealthy person to live with. No way he would walk away from that lifestyle which gave him everything he wanted. I'm not even sure—and I hate to say this because I don't really know for sure—but I'm not sure that his wife even cared about all the affairs. I think she was out there doing her thing, and maybe she was relieved."

Nan looked at her thoughtfully. "It's possible. Of course

we don't always see that aspect of marriage, do we?"

"No, we sure don't," she muttered. "And, when you think about it, if Meredith did care about all the affairs, how many did she know about? Whether she only knew of just one or whether she knew of multiple affairs, at what point in time would she have not liked it?"

"When she was made a laughingstock of the community," Nan replied. "We can all turn a blind eye, but, when we're not allowed to turn a blind eye, we're not allowed to sit in a nice little bubble," she explained, "then that's a whole different story, and that's when people get upset."

Doreen considered that. "You're right. … She might have tolerated a lot, but she wouldn't have tolerated it forever. At some point in time, she would have hit that wall. It's hard to say what they would have done then," Doreen noted. "At the very least, they would have had a pretty ugly fight about it."

"Absolutely," Nan agreed. "When you think about it, what happens in ugly fights?"

"People get hurt," Doreen stated bluntly.

Nan just nodded.

Doreen hated to even think about something like that, and still it didn't mean that a murder had occurred. It certainly didn't mean that anybody had been physically hurt, but words would have flown, and feelings would have definitely vacillated.

Nan got up and announced, "I almost forgot." And she came back out with treats in a basket. Thaddeus was stretching his neck as far as he could to look into the basket.

Doreen stared at her. "What did you do? Raid Richie's stash again?"

Nan chuckled. "Considering he gets all of this because

he says you're coming by, I don't feel bad about going and grabbing a few items for us."

She stared. "He does what?" Her voice rose so high it squeaked. Mugs rolled over to stare up at her, disgruntled at having his nap interrupted. Then the nose shot up and he nudged Nan's knee looking for whatever the smell was.

Nan laughed at her and at Mugs, reaching a hand down to caress his forehead. "Richie is not above making good use of the scenario to get a few extra things for himself," she explained. "Surely you can't begrudge him that."

"I don't begrudge him," Doreen shared, "but I certainly can't say that I'm terribly impressed with the idea of his using me as a scapegoat to get treats."

"Hardly a scapegoat, dear." Nan chuckled. "Fact of the matter is, he likes to have more snacks and to know that he won't starve. And having something like this available for him? … Just part of working the system."

Doreen stared at her, nonplussed. "It never occurred to me that he was getting all these treats in my name, though."

"Since you've become such a big help to the center here," Nan explained, "they are more than happy to share some goodies, so that's not a biggie. What's a couple cookies to them?" She pulled back the tea towel on the basket, and, sure enough, there were six big fat cookies. Nan picked one and said, "We're allowed them all day, so it's hardly an issue."

There wasn't a whole lot Doreen could say to that, but it did make her feel odd. "I would prefer that he didn't do this in my name, though," she repeated.

Nan gave a complacent nod. "Of course you would. On the other hand, he's not hurting anybody."

It was hard to say whether that was true or not, because

Doreen wasn't exactly a resident or a willing participant in this hoarding of food in her name. It definitely did not feel good to hear what Richie was doing, yet Doreen picked up a cookie, looked at it, didn't really want it, and then realized she really wanted it, but she didn't want it because of the way it had been obtained. "If you went down and got cookies right now, would they stop you?" she asked.

"No, of course not," Nan replied. "We are allowed to go get cookies all the time, but you've got to understand. This is just way more fun."

Doreen closed her eyes and groaned. "Is that all it is to you guys, *fun*?"

"Sure, why not?" Nan asked. "We don't have a whole lot else to do. Unless you bring us some more problems to solve."

"Not exactly on my plan for the day," she murmured.

"Right, so this is a good way for Richie to stay busy. Besides, it makes him smile to think that he's getting something for nothing. The fact of the matter is, he pays for it, and he can have it anytime he wants. So he's not getting anything that he wouldn't be allowed."

With that, Doreen had to be happy, and she settled back to enjoy the cookie. "Still does feel a bit wrong."

Nan patted her hand. "It's fine. Don't worry about it."

But, of course, telling her not to worry about it was a whole different story than being able to not worry about it. She sighed and added, "I would much rather that he got things for himself and not because they think I want them. I don't want to have to say something to them."

"Oh, I wouldn't do that," Nan said in alarm. "That would ruin everything."

"Well then, maybe you should tell him to not do it," she

suggested, "before I feel that I have to say something."

Nan frowned at her. "You're such a party pooper."

Doreen laughed. "If that's how you want to look at it, then fine. However, I would much prefer that Richie not use me as his excuse."

"Fine," she said, disgruntled. "But chances are, then you won't get any treats when you come."

"And, if that's the way it is, then that's the way it is," Doreen stated firmly.

Nan shook her head. "You do have a fine set of morals."

"I do," Doreen declared, "and I would like to keep them. Now that you've told me what he's doing, no way in good conscience can I let him continue."

Nan sighed. "Fine. I told Richie that you would be a stick in the mud about it."

"And then why did you let him do it?"

"Because what difference does it make?" she asked. "We pay for them anyway. It's just a game, dear."

And Doreen understood that, but it wasn't much help. She stayed and visited long enough for that unpleasantness to wash away, and then she finally told Nan, "I've got to head home. I'm too tired to function on any kind of decent level right now."

"Well, you're definitely cranky."

Doreen sighed. "Maybe to you that's what it is, and I'm sorry if I've upset you."

Nan said, "Oh, hogwash. I'm not upset. I just know that Richie will find another way to milk the system.'

"Why doesn't he just ask for more cookies, rather than trying to milk the system?"

"Because he's bored, dear. Find us some more puzzles to work on, and he'll be fine."

Doreen shook her head at that. "That isn't quite so easy to do."

"Of course not," Nan agreed, "which is why we're doing what we're doing, anything to help pass the time away." And, with that, she packed up the last two cookies and said, "Here. You might as well take them."

"Why?" she asked warily.

"Because it'll probably be the last ones you get."

Chapter 21

At that, Doreen wasn't even sure what to say, but, with the cookies that Nan insisted she take, Doreen headed home with her animals, slowly walking up the creek, trying to figure out what she was supposed to do about that conversation about Richie. She didn't want anybody taking advantage, particularly in her name.

If he wanted to try and get something for nothing, well, he could do it in somebody else's name, like his own. Yet she also knew she was feeling crankier because she hadn't had enough sleep.

As she wandered up the creek, taking her time, playing with the animals on the way, she was stopped by a couple.

The woman gushed over Mugs. "He is adorable."

Mugs, of course, had to preen and look like he was absolutely perfect, only Thaddeus wasn't happy about being left out. He squawked, popping his head out from behind her hair and squawking again.

The woman squeaked and jumped back. The woman's husband burst out laughing, grabbing his wife as she stumbled. When she finally regained her composure, she shook her head. "My goodness," she murmured. "I certainly wasn't expecting that."

Doreen smiled. "Thaddeus does like to make an entrance," she said affectionately, as she patted the crazy bird on his side.

Thaddeus crowed, "Thaddeus is here. Thaddeus is here."

"Oh my," the woman said in fascination. "He really does talk, doesn't he?"

"He does, and not always when you want him to," Doreen added, with a chuckle. "More often when you don't want him to." At that, Thaddeus gave her the gimlet eye and cried out gently, "Thaddeus loves Nan. Thaddeus loves Nan."

"Yeah, I know," she murmured.

And then he redeemed himself. "Thaddeus loves Doreen."

She smiled, stroked him gently on his head. "As you can see," she told the couple, who were staring at her in fascination, "he's quite a character."

The woman nodded, as if unable to speak. "I never thought they could do something like that." Then she beamed. "Now I know who you are."

Doreen's heart sank, as she slowly nodded. "Maybe you do. My animals do tend to give me away."

The couple chuckled. "I wondered when I saw them, but when Thaddeus started talking," her husband added, "that's a dead giveaway."

"Yes, he has a tendency to let go of all my secrets," she said, with an eye roll.

The other woman smiled. "You really are blessed, you know?"

"I know," Doreen agreed, with a big smile. "The animals, if nothing else, keep my life very enriched in all kinds of ways."

The woman nodded. "That's such a lovely thing to see." She looked over at her husband and linked her arm through his. "We're delighted to have met you. We have been traveling a lot. We live in Southeast Kelowna. But we love to come down here and walk the greenway along the river," she explained, with a smile. "It's nice to see you here."

Doreen nodded. "It's one of my favorite places," she agreed. "Always something is happening."

"As if you don't have enough in your life, where something's always happening," the man noted, with a smile.

She looked over at him. "Southeast Kelowna, *huh*?"

He nodded. "Yes, we live close to"—he stopped, looked over at his wife—"near the food orchard area," he said. "I would say, close to Meredith's place, but that always brings up connotations of what happened so long ago."

"And yet Doreen hasn't been here all that long," his wife replied, "so maybe she doesn't know about that."

"Except that I'm kind of looking into Dennis's case," Doreen murmured.

They looked at her. "Really? Why?"

"Because there've been no answers. Because there's been no progress. Maybe there'll be nothing to find. I don't know."

"Well, you're right about no answers and no progress," the husband replied. "I can't imagine that that's a healthy way for anybody to live."

"Exactly my thoughts," Doreen agreed, "and those two boys."

"Well, they're men now," the husband clarified. "Good men. One's in college down in the US, I believe, although he's probably home over the summer, and the other one works on the farm with his mom."

Doreen nodded. "I've heard absolutely nothing but good things about them."

"And with good reason," the husband noted. "Those boys have been devoted to being there for their mother, and she went through a really rough time, when her husband just upped and disappeared like that."

"It's kind of crazy, isn't it?" Doreen asked. "I haven't been able to think of any motivation for somebody to get up and leave."

"There are all kinds of motivation," the husband noted, looking at her, puzzled.

"I meant, what would cause a man to up and leave his wife, two kids, the farm, bank accounts, everything?" she asked, "especially if he left on his own."

"That's always the big question, isn't it?" he said.

His wife nodded. "For me there is no motivation good enough to do that, unless …" The other woman stopped and hesitated.

"Unless?" Doreen prodded, looking at her.

"Unless he was trying to protect his family."

"I did consider that," Doreen said. "So far I haven't really heard too much about what he was like, outside of his affairs."

At that, the other woman's face pinched. "And you can't listen to hearsay on that. Women chased him terribly."

Doreen stared at her. "That's an interesting viewpoint."

"Why?" she asked.

"I suppose she's already heard all the gossip," her husband suggested.

"I've spoken to women who potentially had affairs with him," Doreen shared, "so I don't know how much of that is actual gossip versus facts at this point."

"You've spoken to some of the women?" The other woman asked in shock. "You mean, it's true?"

"Absolutely," Doreen declared.

"Several of them?" The couple looked at each other and then back at her. "We always believed Dennis when he said that the women were always chasing him and that he had nothing to do with it."

"In that case, he was lying," Doreen noted.

"Do you have proof?" the other woman asked.

"I'm not sure how much proof you need when it comes to something like that," she pointed out, "but I have more or less confirmed two women were involved with Dennis, from the women themselves. Then there was mention of many more women but not by name."

"Wow." The woman took a step back. "That's a bit of a shock. We really trusted him."

"Just because he had a wandering eye doesn't mean that he was a terrible person in every way," Doreen added.

"No, no, of course not, but we, for sure, thought that that would have nothing to do with why he left."

"Well, if you bring in the jealous boyfriends, jealous husbands, and everybody else who might have been involved," Doreen suggested, "motivation certainly comes into play."

The husband eyed her, then nodded slowly. "I'm Michael, and this is my wife, Marla. We did know the couple at the time, but we've been traveling so much that we kind of lost touch with it all. So every time we come back, it feels like it's new and fresh again."

"Whereas the people here have moved on," Marla added, with a nod.

"Because there's been no progress on the case, and that always blew me away too," Michael murmured. "I mean, when you think about it, how far can anybody go to really escape their past?"

"In this day and age, they can go forever. If they have a way to change their identity and have a source of income or a way to have enough money to get up and go," Doreen suggested, "they can disappear."

"It's just not what you would expect from people like that, you know?" Marla noted.

"That's what we're left with," Michael stated in sadness, "because we did know them. I mean, him in particular."

"Did you ever see him with anybody?"

"No, no, of course not," Michael replied, "and that's part of the reason why we didn't believe everything that everybody was saying afterward. I mean, we trusted him because he told us that he wasn't cheating." He looked over at his wife. "You did talk to his wife too, didn't you?"

"I did, and she was pretty upset that I would even listen to the rumors."

"Right," Michael agreed. "It's not what anybody wants to be told about their relationship anyway, so that wouldn't be easy on her."

"Did you talk to her before the disappearance or afterward?" Doreen asked the couple.

"Afterward," Marla replied. "I know I probably shouldn't have. It kind of broke something in our relationship then, that I would even bring it up." She looked apologetically over at her husband.

"We've talked about it among ourselves often since, and there's just no easy answer."

Doreen smiled. "That's the thing. It could take a while,

but eventually the answers do surface. What it takes is for people to open up and to talk honestly. Until that happens, lots of this just stays buried. But being buried isn't a good answer either, and so we wait for people to speak up and to say something."

"Do you find people speaking up and saying something?" Michael asked.

"Not yet, no," Doreen admitted, "but I keep hoping."

He burst out laughing. "Good luck with that. I get that there are probably a lot of people out there who have a lot to say about it, but they won't necessarily have anything useful to say."

"Everybody always has something to say," Doreen agreed, with a smile. "But, as you pointed out, often it's an ax to grind, or a beef to air out, or grievances about how badly they were treated by this guy, particularly when it comes to women and their partners." She was thinking about Adelaide's husband in City Park. But a lot of that becomes just emotional noise, and it's not necessarily the truth, as everybody involved in the situation would see it differently.

"So you have to be careful not to make assumptions." Marla faced her. "I appreciate that you're going about it gently," she began. "I feel pretty devastated for Meredith's part in this. She was the innocent wife, and, although they fought a lot, she was there for her kids the whole time. Everything was for her children."

Doreen nodded. "Particularly the scenario where the husband is off wandering, that's not something you want the kids to find out about."

"Oh." Marla shuddered. "I can't imagine how terrible that would have been for her. Hopefully now that they're adults, they would understand a little more."

"Maybe so," Doreen muttered.

"How did you even come onto this case?" Michael asked her curiously. "Are you just always looking for cold cases?"

"In an earlier cold case, I had been working on a couple who disappeared, so two missing people," she explained, thinking back. "And then I saw a drone footage of Meredith's xeriscaped front garden and, being a bit of a gardener myself, not a good one by any means"—she chuckled—"just somebody who's fascinated by them, I was quite interested in the xeriscape."

At that, Michael smiled. "We have a similar one. I believe Dennis really wanted to put one in, but she was against it."

Doreen nodded. "I did ask her about it afterward, and she told me that it was to honor him and that she was sorry she had held off all this time and figured she could do this one thing to honor his memory for the kids."

Marla added, "That's what I heard from Meredith too. When he disappeared, and they had nothing, no grave, no body, she put that in for the family."

"That's lovely," Doreen said, with a smile. "I think it's important for the people who survive to have a place to go and to say goodbye. So having a garden like that in his memory, … I can understand that." She nodded gently to the two people. "I know quite a few people who do take the ashes of their beloved and spread it out around the tree that they've planted, so that it can create a new generation of life."

The couple nodded. "That's exactly what she was trying to do. It was pretty emotional for her, I know. We stopped in soon afterward, and she was pretty tired and stressed and looked to the world like her heart was broken."

"Of course it was," Michael added.

"How long afterward did she do it?" Doreen asked the couple.

"I don't know exactly. At the time it seemed kind of fast, but I know the kids were really hollering about daddy and wanting to know where he was and what had happened. And she was looking to find some kind of an answer that would appease them."

"Which is never easy," Doreen noted.

"No, definitely not easy, and, in this case, the kids were even more adamant just because they had spent so much time with him."

She smiled and nodded. "All good reasons."

The couple smiled at her. "If you do find answers," Marla added, "it would be lovely if you could let us know."

Doreen laughed. "I'm sure, if I find answers, *everybody* will know."

"Especially now that you have such a fan club and a following," Marla stated.

Doreen shrugged. "I admit that more and more people recognize me and the animals, whenever we're out, … but I don't know about a fan club. Many people aren't always happy with my investigations."

"Why is that?" Marla asked in astonishment.

Doreen smiled. "Because if they happen to be guilty of a scenario that they don't want unearthed, and I come along, and it's probably one of my cases, and I expose it to the world, then those people generally don't appreciate it."

At that, Michael laughed. "Oh, now that"—he waved his hands—"I can totally see. Well, we have nothing to hide, so it's not our problem. But, as he was our neighbor and a good neighbor at that, although, what you just mentioned about him having affairs? Well, that's disturbing, as we had no idea."

"Nobody should accept anything blindly," Doreen noted, with a gentle smile, "especially when it comes to our friends. It's important to just keep their memory alive and to forget about any other rumors that go with it."

Marla looked at her gratefully. "Thank you for that, because really, he was a good man. I don't know about all the rest of this, but everything that we ever saw showed that he was a caring father and a good man."

Doreen nodded. "And that's what you hang on to then. I'm not trying to burst your bubble, but, if the truth winds up to be anything different, then you'll deal with it at that time. Other than that, I wouldn't worry about it. Life happens, and we all move on."

With that said, Doreen added, "Speaking of which, I'll head home." She waved to the couple and headed her animals back home again.

Chapter 22

INSIDE HER HOME now, Doreen wondered about talking to Meredith again. Would she be willing to? Doreen was pushing painful buttons. Pondering it, she sent a text, asking if she could come and look at her xeriscape. Meredith sent back a question mark.

Doreen sighed and phoned her to explain. "I'm a bit of a gardening nut, and I wondered, if I came and just stayed at the front garden, would that bother you? I didn't want to intrude, but I would really like to see it."

"If I can't get rid of you, I might as well get along with you," Meredith conceded in a hard voice. "So come on by. Just don't do any digging. All kinds of utility lines are buried around there that you could disturb."

"No, that's fine," Doreen agreed, "I guess that means you do have some irrigation?"

"We do, but it's not something that we need. It's more of a just-in-case scenario."

"Right. Well, I would love to see it." After the call ended, she packed up the animals and told them, "I don't know where we're going with this one, but I need to take a closer look at it. So behave yourselves, will you please."

She needed to see that drone footage again too. As she drove up to the area, she stopped just outside of the front yard, parked off to the side, quickly sent Mack a text, explaining where she was. Doreen wasn't sure she could find the drone footage again, not even sure how she got that feed to begin with. Then she pocketed her phone, grabbed the two leashes and, with her animals' heads high, sniffing the area, Doreen walked to the front of the house.

Meredith was there waiting for her, and she frowned at her. "You didn't waste any time, did you? I really don't appreciate all this disruption of you interfering in my life."

"I'm sorry for that," Doreen replied, with a nod. "I do understand."

"I wonder if you really do," Meredith countered in a flat tone. "I get it. Everybody's trying to find my husband, but believe me, at this point in time, I'm not sure I care."

"And believe me. At this point in time, I understand that too," Doreen confirmed, with a smile. "I mean, the guy's been gone how long? If he took off on his own, then who wants anything to do with him anyway?"

Meredith gave a surprised nod. "Exactly. I didn't expect you to understand that." She studied the animals, then shook her head, as if she'd seen everything, and so a cat on a leash wasn't worth commenting on.

"I understand all kinds of things." Doreen gave her a reassuring smile. "I'm sorry that you've been through so much."

"I was raised to do a hard day's work and to be proud of it, not to sit here and shirk my responsibilities," she replied. "So, when Dennis disappeared, I just buried myself in work. It kept me focused." She walked one foot away, staring at her land, her hands on her hips. "The problem with being raised that way is nobody else raised the rest of the world that way, and you end up looking like an idiot when your expectations of other people don't work out," she shared. "I'm sure you've heard by now all the rumors about my husband's affairs."

"Rumors?" Doreen asked. Mugs pulled on his leash, straining to be let loose.

Meredith glared at her. "Fine, hardly rumors. You've obviously heard about the affairs."

"Yes, and, for that, I'm sorry."

Meredith waved at Mugs and snapped, "You might as well let him go. He's a dog. Nothing he can hurt here."

Doreen bent to unclip Mugs from his leash. Goliath just lay at her feet, his tail twitching, completely uninterested in exploring. So no need to unleash him just yet. Doreen returned her attention to Meredith and, with quiet understanding, added, "Nothing quite like being made a fool of by someone we love."

Meredith snorted. "I should have divorced him when I first found out, but I thought it was better for the kids this way—except that Dennis obviously didn't care about the kids finding out either. When Dennis went missing, the police looked at me awfully hard, but I didn't have anything to do with it."

Doreen believed Meredith. Still, Doreen had been wrong before. "How did you feel about him at the end?"

"I probably would have divorced him in the next few months, and maybe that was on his mind when he took off. I don't know. Yet I sure didn't want my kids to think this was an acceptable marriage relationship. Whatever Dennis did, he did a good job of it. He took off in a permanent way," she noted bitterly. "And me? … He left me holding the bag." She stared at the xeriscape, looking away from Doreen. "I hate this, you know?"

"The garden?" Doreen turned to watch, as Mugs walked to the center of it and peed. *Ugh.* Still it was better than taking a dump. When he was done, he sniffed around the area, then laid down and dropped his head to his paws.

"Yes, he always wanted to put it in. I didn't see the point of it. We ran a big orchard, so watering wasn't exactly a problematic part of our world," she explained. "Sure, we have river rights, and some years water was a problem, but I put this in to give the kids something to honor their father by, even though a part of me just wanted to say, *Stop it, leave it be.* I used to imagine having a conversation with Dennis, trying to convince myself that *He took off, and we don't care anymore,* but I never could." She stopped, stared up at the sky for a long moment.

"He had me so twisted up in the days before he left. We fought constantly, once I found out about his affair with Adelaide," she said. "I told him that was it, and there were no second chances with me, and he could just take a hike and disappear. He told me at the time that no way was he disappearing. He'd invested too much time and money into this place, and, if anybody would take a walk, it would be me."

"He said that?" Doreen asked, amazed.

"Yeah. I told him exactly what I thought of that idea, and he wasn't very happy when I explained the terms of the inheritance. I guess he didn't know. Apparently I hadn't told him about it before." Meredith laughed. "I didn't think much of it, and he was pretty angry to find out that the farm couldn't be sold and that he wouldn't get anything off me. He was livid."

"I bet he was."

"Now I understand why my father Danny had done what he'd done and my grandfather Johnson before him. They set up the family farm into a family trust. It would always be miserable for a man like Dennis, looking for an easy time instead of having that same work ethic that I was raised by," she pointed out. "So when Dennis took off, I guess I wasn't really surprised. When his truck showed up missing, of course I was grateful that I had reported it because I didn't do anything wrong. I wouldn't because of my kids."

"That would be the worst thing for the kids to find out after the fact," Doreen agreed.

"The trouble was, then the story came out, about all the affairs—some of the affairs," she corrected, "lots of my neighbors didn't want to believe it. And I certainly didn't go out of my way to encourage them to. I mean, why would I?" She stopped and looked out to the farm, gathering herself. "It was bad enough being a laughingstock already," she admitted, "without having to sit here and confirm everybody's suspicions, but it wasn't easy," she murmured. Then she faced Doreen, Meredith's face hardening and her demeanor changing entirely. "So I would really appreciate if you would do what you need to do and then go."

Doreen nodded silently. "Putting the garden in wasn't a bad thing to do."

"No, it was the right thing to do, and unfortunately it was also the right thing to do for the stupid garden too because it saved us on water, and it's flourished," she said on a groan. "Look at it. It's positively glowing. That's another reason I hate it because Dennis was right, darn it. He was right, and it was one more thing that I had to look at and constantly see, even though I don't want anything to do with it or him."

Doreen raised an eyebrow.

"I'm glad he's gone. … Don't get me wrong though. If he's dead, I'm sorry about that, but I didn't have anything to do with it," she noted bitterly. "It's taken me a very long time to stare down all the neighbors and the questions and the suspicious nature of everybody around me, but we're finally here. We're finally to the point of having this be water under the bridge, where I can hold up my head again," she said, almost hysterically. "And then you come along."

Doreen winced. "I get that, and I'm really sorry."

"Not sorry enough though, are you?" Meredith asked, staring. "It's not as if you'll turn around and walk away and forget this, will you?"

Doreen slowly shook her head. "No, I'm not. I can tell you that I don't have any answers yet, and I haven't gotten very far on it, but I have an inkling of what happened though.'

"Even having that is more than what anybody else has had, not that I'm terribly impressed with an *inkling.*"

At that, Doreen smiled at her. "No, and I get that. Give me a chance to figure it out. If we get to the truth, then you will be free and clear."

"Maybe," Meredith muttered, as she looked around. "There's always that fear, you know? The fear that it was somebody you knew. The fear that the same person will come back and take you out too. The way Dennis disappeared? … Just leaving his truck like he just stopped on the side of the road, and somebody picked him at this prearranged spot made me think that it was one of his girlfriends. It always bothered me that I didn't know who it was because the usual suspects were all still in town. And the truck wasn't left where I thought it would be. The family farm covers miles and miles out here, so it's not unusual for any of us to jump in a truck and to travel to another field to do whatever."

"That had to be hard. Not having answers is the worst."

"Exactly. I also worried about every woman in town, wondering who else had had an affair with my husband, yet I just didn't know about it. I wondered about somebody who *did* have an affair with my husband and was unhappy that he kept coming home to me." Meredith shook her head. "Believe me. It doesn't make for good neighbors. It's not the same town it used to be."

"I'm not sure it was ever that town that everybody thought it was," Doreen suggested, "but it's not a bad town. It's just a place. It's the people who make it good or bad."

Meredith gave a bitter laugh. "Easy for you to say. You haven't been the butt of jokes and mockery of everybody around you."

Doreen winced at that. "I certainly won't go into my life history," she began, "but I've been the butt of plenty of jokes. I got dumped for arm candy myself," she muttered, trying to clear the air because she needed Meredith to know that Doreen understood full well the graveness of her situation. "My entire group of highfalutin friends thought it was the best joke ever."

Meredith stared at her in shock.

Doreen nodded. "Yeah, so I do understand some of what you're going through. I, at least, had some closure. Meanwhile I'm still working on that whole divorce thing right now. Who knew that would be a pain in the butt to do."

Meredith laughed. "Divorces are always a pain in the butt. Everybody wants more than they should have, and whoever has it never wants to share," she said. "That just seems to be the rule of life."

"I never really understood that," Doreen admitted, with a smile, "and my friends would all say I was just stupid and naïve." She raised her hands. Mugs woofed from the garden. She sighed. "Come here, Mugs. Come on, boy." And he slowly got up and trundled toward her. She bent down and clipped his leash back on. "So I do understand. It's not an easy path for either of us. But, if we can get answers for you, then I would like to think that maybe some of this would die down." She looked at the garden. "Do you do all your own manual work?"

"Not all of it. Ten years ago my kids were too small. I would have been out here shoveling for days, but my dad helped," she explained, "and we have equipment here. Some of the guys came to do some of the top-rock work. I had a bunch of it delivered. So that's an expense I didn't really have the money for either back then, but what was I supposed to do? Some people thought it was strange because I did it fast, but I also knew Dennis wasn't coming back. Not after the fight we'd had, not after he found out that he wouldn't get anything. It was very much a case of he was done and gone, and I was done and dusted," she quipped, with a smirk. "And it wasn't that fast. I waited for spring to fully set in, and then it was just done."

"When did you break ground?" she asked.

"Dennis had started the garden. He wanted to do it himself. Then it was a bone of contention between us, so he started it and stopped. He was good at that. He was good at initiating projects and then not completing them. He never saw much through," she muttered. "So the garden was already churned up, and I just finished it. Only over time did it become a memorial." She shook her head. "Do what you need to do. I've got to get back to work."

"Where's your dad now?"

"He lives in the house over there." She waved to her left. "It's still all part of the same property. He gets to stay there for life."

"Is that something your husband could have stopped?"

"Not while I was alive," Meredith declared, with a laugh. "My family members are very close and very strong on doing what each other needs to survive, so no. He couldn't have messed that up."

"Were your parents happy when you married him?" Doreen asked.

Meredith considered that before speaking. "They weren't unhappy. They were absolutely ecstatic when their grandsons were born, but then that's the family dynasty, isn't it? Carrying on the family line," she said, with a smile, "and *that* they were definitely happy about. The rest of it? I don't know. I don't know if they knew about the affairs. I deliberately didn't mention them. I could only handle so many things, and knowing that my family may have all heard about those affairs just doesn't do it for me." She shuddered. "Much better if I could have just not had anybody find out."

"Hiding your head in the sand doesn't generally work," Doreen offered.

Meredith stared at her. "It should. I didn't do anything to deserve this. I didn't need to have all that mockery in my life," she stated flatly. "It's not fair."

"So much in life isn't fair, and I'm sorry for what you went through," Doreen replied. "Hopefully we can get this completely done and dusted, and you can move on with your life."

Meredith slowly nodded. "That's what's missing. I haven't been able to move on. Every time I turn around, I expect him to come through the door, and I still get into the fighting spirit because of the way we ended it." She grimaced. "If he came back now, I would slam the door in his face and call the police. I don't think he wants that either, so I know he's not coming back."

"Maybe he will."

"*Nah*. I knew it back then. I don't know how I knew it. I just knew it. It was one of those inner instinctive feelings, knowing that he would never come home again. While everybody else expressed all the appropriate sympathy, telling me that it was okay, that he would show up again, I couldn't tell any one of them that I was ecstatic he was gone and that I hoped he stayed gone. Nobody would understand, and I was already being looked at sideways, wondering if I had killed him, but I didn't kill him. I didn't kill him," she cried out, with rising hysteria, "but I sure wanted to. For what he did to me, to my kids, for making me the laughingstock and for making his kids find out about him, but I didn't." And, with that, she looked over at Doreen, a wild look in her eyes, and repeated, "So hurry up and do whatever you've got to do, and then please just get out of here and leave me alone." And, with that, Meredith raced into the house.

Chapter 23

DOREEN STAYED FOR a little bit longer, as she studied the xeriscape and looked at the dimensions and along the sides. The animals walked quietly at her side. She wanted the drone view to confirm her suspicions, and she also needed to talk to Meredith's father and her grandfather and a few other people yet. She also knew it would be a much harder scenario to get the answers she wanted.

With Mugs on a leash, she stayed on the side of the garden and just studied the plants. When she was finally done, satisfied with what she saw, or at least satisfied with what was here, she turned, and, with a wave up at the window, she headed back to her vehicle. If nothing else, she could get out of the woman's hair and give Meredith some peace. Not that she would find any peace in all this meddling in her life.

Doreen drove up to the next property on the lot, where her father lived. As Doreen got out, an old man sat on the front porch in a rocking chair. He looked at her and just kept rocking. "Hey. My name's Doreen."

"I know who you are," he spat in a hard voice. "You're trouble. That's what you really are."

Doreen winced. "I can't say that I've been told that very

often quite so bluntly."

"Oh, you're trouble all right," he repeated. "You're the kind who comes in with a smile and pretty hair and all that sunshine and roses, and, next thing you know, a man's all tied up in knots. You're that kind of trouble."

Doreen stared at him. "I'm not that kind of trouble," she declared. "I don't have affairs with married men. I don't have affairs with anybody I don't know is free and clear, and I'm still dealing with a divorce myself. So it's not as if I'm in any position to make trouble where there isn't any."

He nodded. "Yeah, say whatever suits you, but I know what you are. You're trouble."

Doreen didn't know what she could say to convince him otherwise, so she dropped that subject. "I came to ask you about your daughter's xeriscape garden."

"Yeah, trouble," he repeated, with a nod.

"I'm not sure what kind of trouble that is."

He just stared at her.

"Are you Meredith's father?" Doreen asked him.

He snorted. "I'm Johnson, Meredith's grandfather." He shook his head. "But thanks for the compliment." He called to the open door, "Hey, Danny Boy, get your butt out here." At that, another older man, but not quite as old, stepped through the doorway and looked at her enquiringly.

She smiled. "Hi."

"She's trouble," Johnson said immediately.

Danny stared down at him. "You say that about everybody nowadays."

"Well, this one's trouble," Johnson repeated. "I wouldn't talk to her, if I were you."

Danny looked at her in surprise.

She shrugged. "I'm Doreen, and I'm looking into the

disappearance of your son-in-law."

His face hardened. "That no-good, worthless excuse of a human? He made a laughingstock out of my daughter, and all she ever did was work hard for him, and that's how he treated her?" He shook his head in disgust.

"I get that. Nobody in your family is particularly bothered about his disappearance."

"Good riddance, as far as I'm concerned," Danny declared in a laconic tone. "What's this got to do with you anyway?"

"Trouble," Johnson muttered off to the side. He spat some chew out of his mouth. "She ain't nothing but trouble, Danny Boy."

Doreen was getting a little tired of hearing that. "I'm hardly trouble, *unless* you've done something wrong, and then maybe I am trouble." She shrugged. "Just because I'm here looking at this missing person's case doesn't make me anything but someone who might close this book for good. I've already spoken to Meredith, and I was asking some questions about the xeriscape. She told me that you were the one who put it in."

"I did part of it," Danny confirmed. "My dad here did a bunch of it as well. Then so did that useless son-in-law. He ripped up the ground, then left it as a big eyesore, probably to piss us off too. He did half-finished jobs like that all too often. So, it was one thing we could do for her, when he left. Get rid of yet another ugly reminder. We were trying to find closure for the grandsons too, and they wanted it done because their father had left it unfinished, when he upped and went off to God-knows-where. Never knew how often that he had left everything undone, including his zippers," Danny said, with a snort.

"I'm sorry. She's had a tough time of it."

"She has, indeed. So why do you want to go stir it all up again?" Danny asked in disbelief.

"I just thought maybe the kids would like to have some answers."

"Well, those kids are men now," he stated, "and they've come to terms with the fact that their father just buggered off."

She stared at him. "Even if that's not true?"

His eyebrows shot up toward his hairline. "Do you have any idea what happened?" he asked.

"No, I really don't."

"See? She's just trouble," Johnson repeated, with a hard glare.

She looked over at him, trying to keep her temper. "I don't consider myself trouble."

"Yeah, you're trouble," Johnson muttered, and he just kept repeating it.

She looked over at Danny, staring down at his father, a note of resignation in his gaze. "I'm sorry." She pointed at Johnson.

Danny nodded. "Apparently it's what happens to all of us when we get to that advanced age. We go dotty."

"I'm not dotty," Johnson snapped. "She's trouble."

"Maybe she is, and maybe she isn't, but she's here right now. So I need to answer her questions then she can leave."

At that, Johnson looked over at her. "Or she can just leave now."

Danny winced. "I'm sorry," he told Doreen. "Obviously it's not a great time to talk."

"I can see that," she agreed, yet she hesitated. "I just wondered when you put in the xeriscape garden and why you put in the piping underneath."

"Because we weren't sure how it would work," Danny explained. "This area is really unpredictable. We can have a lot of water, and sometimes we have no water. New springs can pop up on a day-to-day basis, and you have to pipe it over to a ditch, and not every place has a ditch. Then you can have years when there is no water." He shrugged. "It just seemed, if we would put it in, and to ensure we didn't have to dig it up any more than we wanted to, prudent to put in irrigation lines at the same time."

"Right." She nodded. "And how long after his disappearance did that happen?"

He just stared at her. "Maybe only a few weeks. I don't know exactly when though. We all kept waiting for him to come home, even though his truck was missing and then was found, but nobody had any answers about him." Danny showed his palms. "I know the kids were headstrong, crying, and they were just staring at the garden, asking when Daddy was coming home to fix it. The garden itself seemed to be an issue. And we decided that we needed to turn it into something that would be less traumatic for them and that would honor their father."

"Aah."

"Yeah, just because I didn't like the sorry excuse for a man," Danny replied, "that didn't mean that my grandkids didn't deserve to have some good memories."

"Of course not," she agreed. She looked over at Johnson, still muttering about *trouble*. "Did you use equipment to dig it up?"

Danny laughed. "When you have equipment, you use equipment," he stated. "And, when you have equipment, generally you don't ever choose to go back to having no equipment." She stared at him for a moment. He added to clarify, "Meaning that anytime we can do something with equipment, we do it with equipment. Why wouldn't we?"

"Ah, sorry. I was not trying to be dense."

At that, Johnson snorted. "She's just trouble."

She looked over at the older man. "It would be nice if you decided that I wasn't trouble."

"*Trouble*," Johnson repeated, with a headshake. "You're just trouble."

She winced. "Is it all women or just me?" she asked Danny.

"At this point in time, it's mostly all women," Danny said, with a heavy sigh. "So don't take it personally."

She smiled at him. "I won't. Enough things are going on in life that make him a nonissue for me."

"Good," Danny said. "Anyway, I don't know what else I can tell you. The garden is doing quite well," he pointed out. "Lots of times when I go over there, it's the first thing I see, and I think we did the right thing," he added honestly. "We took something that was bad and ugly, and we made it into something nice."

She smiled. "I really like that idea."

"See? Trouble," Johnson mentioned once again.

She stared at him. "Are you just being cranky?"

Johnson glared at her some more.

At that, Danny suggested, "I'm sorry. Can I ask you to leave now, please? Otherwise he'll just get worse."

"Of course, yes. Sorry, didn't mean to set him off."

"It doesn't take much to set him off these days," Danny noted.

She smiled. "What kind of equipment did you use?" she asked, as they walked back over to her vehicle.

Danny frowned at her. "I don't know why you care about the equipment," he stated, "but we have tractors, backhoes, and diggers. We have it all."

She nodded. "So the garden wouldn't have taken all that much effort."

"No, not at all," he agreed, "and that just made it easier to do, and the only thing we cared about was doing the right thing for the boys."

"I haven't met either of the boys yet."

"One is at university down on the coast, and the other one works on the farm, with his mom."

"I guess it was pretty traumatizing for them, wasn't it?"

"Just think about it from their perspective," Danny began. "You go to bed one night, and your dad's there, and you wake up, and you never see him again. And, in this case, their parents had had a bad fight, and the kids had heard it, so that brought all kinds of extra trauma to the family."

"Oh, ouch," she murmured. "I can see how that would be rather hard."

"It absolutely was hard," he confirmed, "and you do what you can do, but you can't always solve everything for everybody all the time."

"Words to live by. Thank you." And, with that, she headed back to her car and headed home.

Chapter 24

DOREEN DROVE HOME, her mind full of thoughts, ideas, options, all kinds of theories running through her head, and yet nothing was really workable yet. She now had more people to look at, and she really wished she would get a chance to speak with the kids, but, of course, nobody would let her do that. She pulled up to the nearby corner store, where she'd shopped a couple times already. It was a unique little place, and they had a little coffee corner.

With the fresh coffee in her hand, she paid for it and stepped back out again and walked to her car, then looked around. A young man stood beside a pickup truck, thumbing through a bunch of mail. Even though he rested against his truck and wasn't standing fully upright, he appeared to be very tall and big for his age. He looked over at her and smiled.

"Hey," she greeted him. "Beautiful day, isn't it?"

He shrugged. "When you live here, every day is a beautiful day."

She smiled. "I really like hearing that. Too often people have the opposite attitude."

"But that's an attitude," he pointed out, chuckling.

"When you've had bad days, you learn to recognize the good days, and I determined that I would only have good days from now on."

She smiled. "That's a really good way to go through life."

He shrugged. "Either you make it happen or you don't. Are you new here?"

"I moved to Kelowna a little over six months ago." She cast her mind back, her eyes widening. "Wow, the time is going by so fast."

He laughed. "That's always the case, especially when you're having fun." He looked at the animals and nodded. "Having a dog is a good idea."

"And a cat and a bird," she added, with an eye roll.

"A bird?"

At that, Thaddeus squawked through the partially opened car window and cried out, "Thaddeus is here. Thaddeus is here."

He walked closer and took one look at the carload of animals, and he started to laugh. "Okay, now you may have taken things a little too far."

She grinned at him. "Or maybe not far enough. This is kind of a test."

He shook his head. "As long as you keep them long-term," he noted. "Nothing worse than a pet owner who takes them on because it looks like a fun job and then walks away before they have a chance to see how it'll be long-term. Then the animals are tossed into the soup yet again."

"That's not my style," she stated. "I care too much about my pets."

"Good," he muttered. "That's the way it's supposed to be." He shook his head at Thaddeus. "He talks, *huh*?"

"Always at the wrong moments," she muttered.

"Big Guy, Big Guy," Thaddeus said, as he tried to scratch at the window. She opened the door.

The young guy said, "Wait, wait. Won't it fly away?"

At that, Thaddeus jumped onto her hand and crawled up to her shoulder.

"No, he likes being carried around too much," she shared, with a smile.

"Wow." The young man considered Thaddeus. "That's pretty amazing."

"He's pretty amazing," she agreed. "He's a full-on character."

"It's better than being a nonentity," he declared. "When you go through parts of life, frozen, wondering when the next blowup will happen, … looking around the corner for something to happen that never does, you learn to get up and go deal with it, or you become just kind of a ghost, who walks through life," he shared. "My brother and I had a bit of a shock a few years back, and it was all we could do to get through it because we kept looking for this family member who went missing to come back."

She stared at him. "I'm sorry to hear that. Are you talking about Dennis Polanski?"

He nodded, frowning at her. "You've heard of that case? Most people don't appreciate having it brought up."

"No, I'm sure that's very true," she agreed. She hesitated and then decided honesty was the best medicine. "I've been looking into it."

He stared at her. "Why?" And now suspicion was in his voice.

She sighed. "Definitely not to upset you and your family. My thoughts were more along the line, … isn't it time for closure?"

"Oh, it's past time," he confirmed, still staring at her. Then he frowned, looked at the bird, looked back at her, and she knew what was coming. "You're the one who solves those cases."

She winced and nodded. "So far I've been lucky enough to make a difference to many families, yes. Obviously that good luck streak could die at any time."

He nodded, but some of the suspicion in his gaze eased back. "I wouldn't be against your solving it, though," he replied. "It's been a long time to go without answers. … We were forced to pick up and to move on, but I'm not kidding about always turning around, looking for him, expecting him to show up from one day to the next. At this point I know it won't happen, but that doesn't stop the child inside me from looking to see if it will happen."

"I get that," she replied, with full understanding. "I don't think you can ever go through a loss like that without wondering and worrying over what might have happened."

"Maybe so, but … How do you walk away from family? How do you walk away from somebody you love? Somebody who was there for us all the time," he shared. "The rumors afterward were pretty ugly too."

She winced and nodded. "I have to admit I have heard a few of them."

He snorted. "Everybody loves to smear somebody who's not around to defend himself. But it's not true. None of it is true."

"None of what's true?" she asked, tilting her head, wondering just how much he did know.

"He loved my mom," he declared. "I know he did."

But, of course, he was a child back then and seeing

things from a child's point of view, and love was a very complicated thing.

"You'll hear all kinds of stuff if you go down that pathway," he stated, frowning. "Most people didn't have a whole lot of good to say about him."

"That's not very nice at all."

"No, it's not nice, but people will be people."

"I can't argue with that. You are an adult now," she noted. "Are you sure the rumors aren't true?"

He glared at her, but then his shoulders sagged. "I don't want them to be true, and, as long as I don't have to examine them, I don't have to hear them again. So I can believe what I want."

"He's your father. You should keep good memories of him," she suggested. "So I would say this once. None of the rumors need to change that, regardless if it's the truth."

"Yet he didn't come back," he muttered, bitterness rolling out of him.

"And we need to know why."

He nodded. "I'm not against you getting answers, but I hope you don't rake up all that mess."

"I'll do my best," she replied, "but there are a few questions I might have to ask, and a few questions you might not like if I do ask them."

He stared at her for a long moment, and she could see the child inside warring with the man. "I've had several relationships at this point in my life. My girlfriend and I are looking at getting married," he shared. "I would like to know, and I would like to not have to carry all that forward into a relationship that really shouldn't have this kind of history attached to it."

"It's only attached if you let it be," she murmured.

He gave her a boyish grin. "That doesn't help much when you're dealing with this kind of loss. So, based on that, what would you like to know?"

"I was asking about the xeriscape garden in front of your place. It's pretty special."

He nodded proudly. "My great-grandpa Johnson—well, all of us," he corrected, "worked on it. But really my grandpa Danny put that together for us. We needed a place to talk to my dad, a place to just remember him in a good way and to not be part of that whole nasty storm that was brewing around us."

"Was anybody in particular spreading rumors?"

"One guy attacked my dad, and he went to jail, and, when he got out, all he kept saying about my dad's disappearance was *good riddance*."

"Right. I did hear something about him."

"Yeah, you should look at him, if you think my dad's been killed. Believe me. ... I took a serious look at him myself, but I never had any way to prove anything."

"And proof is very necessary," she said. "We can't convict people on the basis of previous actions. It has to be something concrete."

He shrugged. "I was pretty okay with punching this guy out and not having too much proof." Then he gave her that grin again. "But seriously, if you can do this, we will all really appreciate it."

She nodded slowly. "I hope that's the case when I get there," she noted, "because it may not turn out to be anything that you would like to hear."

His expression turned serious, and he nodded. "I know. Believe me. I know, but my brother and I? We talked about it several times, and it is something that we would like cleared up. We want the truth, even if he's dead. And if he was killed by somebody we know?" His hands fisted in front of her.

"Then you will deal with it mentally and emotionally and mourn as a family," she stated, "but you can't get into further trouble. That would hurt your mother. Just let the law handle it."

He stared at her. "Of course I will."

She gave him a ghost of a smile. "You almost made that sound believable."

He burst out laughing. "If you know about the xeriscape garden, have you talked to my mom?"

"I have, indeed. She knows that I'm doing this."

"How did she take it?" he asked cautiously.

Doreen contemplated what to say and then spoke. "I think she would like it to be done and to have answers and to already be on the other side of this process. I can't say that she is happy with me though. She wants to protect you and your brother from further bad news."

He stared at her and then gave a quick nod. "And that does tell me a lot, and it's very much what she would say. I know it's been a trial for her. She hasn't let herself have another relationship, nothing at all, even friends with another man, just because she didn't feel that she could trust anyone."

"And yet you keep telling me that Dennis was a good guy."

He flushed. "Yeah. The difference in viewpoint from a child and from the wife. I heard the rumors too. I don't want to believe them, and a part of me won't even examine whether they are true or not, but I know there's got to be a reason why Mom won't have another relationship."

"Maybe, if we can clear this up," Doreen suggested, "we can free her up to find happiness again."

He studied her for a long moment, looked again at her animals, and finally said, "Well, good luck. ... I'll give you my phone number. If you have any questions, maybe contact me and not my mom. I would like to minimize her pain. I'm supposed to be the man in the family now." He gave a headshake. "That's not an easy thing to be when you don't have answers. You kind of go on blind faith that it all works out the way it's got to work out." He shook his head. "Still, answers would be good."

"They'll be good if nothing else because of the next generation coming up."

He flashed her a surprised look. "How do you know my girlfriend's pregnant?"

She chuckled. "I didn't know, but now that we *do* know, it's even more important to get this settled. Let's not carry this kind of pain through another generation."

"Agreed."

And, with his phone number now tucked securely into her wallet, she headed back to her car, opened it up, and got in. He watched her until she backed away and drove off. She didn't recognize the truck. It was more of a blue-gray kind of a color, not black like the newer one or the beat-up one that had come around her place. However, she wasn't a fool and didn't really trust anyone yet. Plus Doreen knew a farm of that size and with all those employees would have multiple trucks at their disposal.

This son seemed sincere, and his heart seemed to be in the right place, and he was willing to deal with Doreen to supposedly help his mother. Still, Doreen wouldn't trust too early.

Chapter 25

ALL THE WAY home, Doreen found herself looking behind her, checking to see if she was being followed. But when it was clear, she breathed a sigh of relief. She whipped up to her driveway and into her garage, quickly hoping that nobody else would pop into the area. She closed the garage door, watching outside until she couldn't any longer.

As soon as she walked inside the house, she carried through to the kitchen and opened up the door to the backyard. "Time to sit outside and relax," she announced cheerfully.

Mugs raced outside and started barking like crazy. She groaned and stepped outside.

Nobody was there, but something was written on the deck. She stepped closer to read it. *Stay away, you nosy busybody.*

She stared at it, and her first thought was anger because of her beautiful deck. And her second thought was, *Wow, I've really upset somebody.* She quickly took a photo of it and sent it to Mack. He phoned her immediately.

"Is that your deck?" he asked.

"Yes, it is."

"I'm on my way." And he ended the call.

She smiled at that. If nothing else, she at least had somebody on her side through all this. Although she was pretty sure Mack would still be angry that someone was bothering her.

She kept the animals off the deck, as she studied the paint. Would it wash off or would she have to scrape it off and refinish her deck?

Swearing to herself, she went inside, put on coffee, and, still upset, she stood at the open doorway and studied the area. Who did this? Yet the only thing that she could think about was her current case, although Mack would very quickly point out that it could have been somebody from any one of her most recent cases because she had a tendency to upset people with her questions. Roscoe's case had been the last one. However, she didn't think he would have anything to do with this vandalizing of her deck, and they'd caught the killer in that case.

Pondering this, without trying to stare too much at the actual damage to her deck, she waited to hear Mack's truck, then raced to the front window. She opened the curtain cautiously and stared out to make sure it was him, and, when it was, she opened up the front door and let Mugs race to him. And maybe because he hadn't seen him for a little bit, Mugs's enthusiasm in seeing Mack was way over-the-top. By the time she managed to calm down Mugs, and Mack was still chuckling from Mugs's greeting, Mack straightened and then all the laughter stopped.

"When did you first see it?" he asked briskly, as he headed toward the kitchen, then to the deck.

"Just before I texted you," she said.

He didn't say anything, just nodded. "It could be all kinds of things, but obviously you've rattled somebody's cage again."

"Yeah, ya think?" she muttered.

He looked over at her and asked, "What case?"

She shrugged. "The same one."

He nodded. "So it looks like maybe it was a murder, *huh?*"

"I don't know. It seems way too easy to jump to murder at this point."

"Easy?" He stared at her.

"Maybe not easy," she corrected, "but simple." He just shot her a look, headed out to the backyard, looking for any sign of anybody else who had been here. When he turned and called out to Richard, Richard's head popped over the fence, and he glared at Mack.

"Most cops would come to the front door."

Mack stared at him, his hands on his hips. "Did you hear anybody in the backyard in the last while?" Richard opened his mouth to give him a smart-aleck answer, and then he saw the paint all over Doreen's deck. His smart answer fled, and he gasped. "Oh no, not the deck," he cried out.

"Yeah, the deck," Mack stated, his tone grim. "So answer my question."

Richard shook his head. "No, I didn't. Honest I didn't hear anybody."

"Too bad," Mack snapped, "because Doreen wasn't here, and someone obviously took advantage." He turned and raised an eyebrow at Doreen.

She checked her watch and said, "I've been gone two hours."

After Mack did a hard perusal of her entire backyard, he had another conversation with Richard, which didn't appear to net any further information, Doreen went inside, and poured two cups of coffee, and sat on the kitchen step.

Mack sat down beside her. "Any ideas who you pissed off?"

She glared at him.

He just cracked a grin. "Hey, I know you didn't do it on purpose."

"No, I didn't do it on purpose," she declared, "but obviously some people out there are a little perturbed at me."

He raised an eyebrow and smirked. "Ya think?"

She sighed. "I mean, it's to be expected, right? I go in, and I rustled some feathers, and people don't like that." It was a credit to him that he didn't say anything about her wording. "Fine, I know I didn't say that very well." She raised both hands. "Feel free to laugh."

He shook his head. "I won't laugh at you. You're trying your hardest to verbalize how you feel. Considering what you've just been through, I won't say anything."

She looked at him suspiciously, but he seemed sincere. Her shoulders sagged. "And this vandalism isn't even very much mischief to have been through, right?"

"We're not in a contest," he replied. "Somebody has once again violated your space, and that will rend some reaction within you."

"Yeah, I would like to punch him," she said instantly. Mack's grin flashed and then disappeared. "I know. I'm not a violent person, but there are times …"

"There are, indeed, times," Mack agreed, "but that doesn't help us solve who would have done this."

"No, and I really don't have any ideas."

"Who were you talking to today?" She went over it with him. "Interesting," he muttered. "I did talk to both of those men back then too. … Danny was particularly affable and friendly. I didn't speak with the kids though. And the kids' great-grandfather Johnson was very protective of the kids."

"Wow, you're male, and I'm female. You're official, and I'm not. The kids' great-grandfather Johnson kept saying I was nothing but trouble."

Mack stared at her. "To your face?"

"Oh, yeah, to my face, over and over and over again."

"I wonder what that was about."

"His son openly spoke about his father's mental decline, and Danny did ask me to leave, but he did it nicely, saying that his father would just go in a downward slide of a rampage if I didn't. So, if I was hoping he would get better, and I could ask him any questions, I could forget that."

He nodded. "I imagine that that's got to be hard. Some people, when they develop Alzheimer's, get aggressive and ugly, and then the person you once knew is no longer there. That could very well be what's happening there."

"I don't know. I can't say I really want to know either," she muttered, lost in her thoughts, "because that would have to come from firsthand experience, which I don't want Nan to go through, or me either. I love Nan and her sharp wit, even though sometimes I think she's losing it."

"That's okay," Mack said instantly. "I'm pretty sure she thinks you're losing it too."

She stared at him and then burst out laughing at his comment. "Isn't that the truth? And, yes, you've succeeded."

"Succeeded in what?" he asked sweetly.

"Making me feel better," she admitted with a sigh, while glaring at him.

"I just wasn't certain how you were feeling, and I wanted to ensure at least some open honesty was involved in it."

She nodded. "I get that."

"I also get that you're a little too smart for anyone's good." He just stared at her.

She shrugged. "Just an opinion, mind you."

He rolled his eyes. "Just an opinion? Thanks for that."

"You're welcome," she said magnanimously. "I really do appreciate who you are, though." He didn't say anything, so she continued. "You do treat me well, and you tolerate a lot."

At that, he nodded. When she glared at him, he smiled, and held up his hands in surrender. "What do we do from here is the question. That's really what we need to focus on."

"Do you think this will escalate?" she asked him.

"This has more of a childhood prank feel to it, but that doesn't mean that it won't escalate into something much more serious."

Glumly she stared at the writing. "When I saw it, you know what my first thought was?"

"No, what?" he asked.

She stared at him. "That they damaged my deck, and I didn't know how to fix it. That they ruined something so special and maybe forever."

He looked at the deck and nodded. "I guess I understand that. It's a beautiful deck."

"It was a beautiful deck, and I know that it was so hard to come by, and it took a lot of people to make it happen," she said, tears collecting in her eyes. "The thought of losing it …"

"You won't lose it," he said instantly. "This is very fixable." He hopped up to his feet. "I've got a forensic team coming. They'll take a closer look, and we can see what they say. In the meantime, I'll go in and make a sandwich," and, with that, he walked inside.

She stared after him. She got up and asked, "Did I say something wrong?"

He turned toward her and frowned. "No, you didn't say anything wrong, and I'm coming inside to do something, so that I don't say anything wrong." He turned back to the fridge, gathering ingredients for his sandwich.

She didn't get it. She stared at him and frowned. "I feel like this is one of those unwritten rules about relationships, and I don't know what the rule is." He turned again and raised an eyebrow. She shrugged. "I feel like I've done something wrong." His jaw had that tic working now.

"The thing is, you don't know what you've done wrong. So, because you don't know what you've done wrong, and because to you it's not necessarily wrong, it doesn't really leave me with anything that I can say."

"Oh, so this is one of *those* kind of talks."

He sighed. "It's hard for me to let you just go off and raise all kinds of mischief, knowing that people come after you in retaliation. It's hard to sleep at night, wondering if somebody will come back in the night after you. It's hard to let you get up tomorrow and do it all over again. However, it's your right. Still, that doesn't mean it's easy for me."

"Sometimes it is like that for me too, where you are concerned," she shared.

He nodded. "That's why I came in here, so I don't say something because I know that, even if I do say something, you won't quit."

"No, I won't," she said slowly.

"So that's why I'm not saying something." And he went

back to pulling out bread and looking for meat.

"A bit of ham is in the crisper," she murmured absentmindedly.

He nodded, pulled it out. "I'll replace it today or tomorrow."

"Don't worry about it. You buy enough groceries for here." She sat down at the kitchen table, knowing that she was supposed to say something but not sure how to make it come out right. "A part of me says I should apologize," she finally said.

He stopped and looked at her. "A part of you? Apologize for what?"

"That's the problem," she admitted. "I'm afraid the apology is more to do with what my husband would expect, and, therefore, I won't apologize." The mention of Mathew earned her another tic in his jaw.

"That's good," he replied, "because you know how I feel about being compared to your ex."

"Oh, I certainly wouldn't ever compare you to him," she replied cautiously. "There are similarities between him and all males, so it's not a *him* thing. It's a *men* thing. And, of course, you don't want to see me get into trouble that I can't handle, and your experience says there's an awful lot of trouble out there that I have yet to see. So, chances are, I'll come up against something that I won't get out of quite so easily, and you don't want that to happen."

He stopped and stared. And then nodded, while slathering mayonnaise all over the bread. She winced at the amount of mayo that he was putting on there. "You sure you don't want to put something other than mayonnaise on there?"

He just glared at her and kept working on it.

"Apparently I have stirred up things, and somebody is

upset at me."

He gave another quick nod. "Go on."

She sighed. "That's making you even angrier. So I'm not helping right now."

"Tell me more," he said.

She thought about it and then shrugged. "Maybe you're just trying to deal with the fact that this is a dangerous situation and that you can't control me."

"I'm not trying to control you," he corrected, shooting her a look.

"No, you're not," she agreed, and then she beamed at him. "See? You're doing so much better at this than I am."

He stopped, let out a heavy sigh. "Doesn't feel like it. You know if I had any way to make it happen, I would order you completely away from all this."

She nodded. "You won't do that because you know that you don't have that right. Plus you don't want to see how I would react because that, of course, is something that my ex would have done. You're afraid that I might have fallen back into the same habits, and I would obey you—which would make you happy and at the same time very upset."

He stared at her, blinked several times, and then a slow grin washed across his face. "You have a very interesting turn of phrase. I'll give you full credit for that and say yes."

She nodded. "I get that. I'm really not trying to do something that would get me in trouble. You know that, right?"

"And yet it happens just so easily," he muttered, staring at her, with that one eyebrow raised.

She couldn't argue with that. It was true. It seemed as if trouble just found her, even though she wasn't doing anything. "Not sure what I'm supposed to do about that though," she admitted. "Again, I'm not … I'm not trying to go against *anybody's* wishes. There was no need for somebody to come after me on this case. The fact that somebody did …"

He nodded. "Which is another reason why I'm not saying what is bubbling up inside my head."

She gave him a misty smile. "Because you also know that this means that somebody's upset, and somebody is getting antsy, and that's good for us. Isn't it?"

"Well, it's good for me," he clarified, once again stopping and looking at her. "I'm not so sure it's good for you."

"You really think he's after me?"

"I don't know," he admitted. "How can we take a chance and be wrong?"

She winced at that. "Okay, I can see that too. That's not exactly how I wanted this conversation to go."

"I'm sure you didn't," he said, as he slapped ham atop the mayo and then started slicing cheese with vigor, revealing he was still quite upset. "Still, it's also interesting because we didn't have anything to go on. So who are you upsetting, and why are they upset?"

"I would have to say they're upset because they had something to do with Dennis's disappearance. If we could find out who's following me around or doing this," she suggested, "that would help a lot."

"Would it though?" Mack asked. "People do these kinds of things for all kinds of reasons, and a lot of the time they aren't for any reasons that make any sense to us."

"Right, so it even could be the husband of the woman that I met downtown, Adelaide's husband."

He tilted his head and stared at her. "I suppose it could be, particularly if you weren't responding to him in the way he wanted you to."

"Responding to him?"

"If he was warning you off and trying to get you to stop doing something or whatever. And you weren't responding in the right way."

"Right." She frowned, then nodded. "Yeah, he didn't look very happy with me."

At that, Mack gave a snort and then added the punctuation of an eye roll.

She grinned at him. "You have a very expressive face."

"I do with you," he said, as he picked up one of his sandwiches, without cutting it, and took a huge bite out of it. Chewing furiously, he glared at her.

She waited until he swallowed, and then she walked over, wrapped her arms around him, and laid her head against his chest. "It's really hard for you, isn't it?" She tilted her head back, and he nodded, staring down at her with a look she didn't recognize. Yet his free hand was wrapped around her and holding her tight. But it was a look that she really wanted to recognize. Because it revealed so much about him. "I'll be careful, you know?"

He shoved another huge bite of sandwich into his mouth and glared at her but continued to squeeze her tightly against him.

She smiled. "I'm really proud of you."

He shook his head at that.

"I am. You haven't reamed me out. You haven't told me to stay in the house, *like a little woman should*. You haven't done any of those major faux pas," she added, with emphasis.

He rolled his eyes at her.

"Matter of fact, I think you're doing very well."

He swallowed again and sighed. "I'm calm. You don't

have to keep buttering me up."

"Oh, good. So you won't be upset if I poke the bear again?" When he glared at her, she shrugged. "You know it's about the best way to make something happen."

"It's also the most dangerous way."

"Agreed, but wouldn't it be nice if these guys would turn out to be nice people instead of the jerks that they are showing themselves to be?"

"Who?" he asked, with a note of humor. "Guys facing life sentences for murder? … Yeah, they'll do everything they can to fight you."

"So far we're winning the battle," she noted cheerfully. "Me and my trusty little team."

At that, he glared at her again.

"We have been doing just fine, and, yes, I know," she admitted. "It won't always be that way."

He sighed. "No, it won't be. I just hope I'm there to pick up the pieces when you fall."

"I hope you're there *before* I fall, and so picking up the pieces is an easy job."

"Me too," he muttered, "but I'm not holding my breath."

Chapter 26

MACK FINISHED HIS sandwich as his team arrived. After checking on the damage and looking for any clues the forensic team had left, and Mack left with them. Doreen was exhausted. Then almost as if she had a spy close by, Nan called her.

"What happened?" she cried out. "You had the police at your place again?"

Doreen groaned. "Somebody decided to spray a warning all over my beautiful deck."

"Oh no," she cried out, "not the deck."

"Yeah, the deck," Doreen muttered. "I feel really bad about that."

"Why should you feel bad about that?" Nan asked indignantly. "You didn't spray paint it, … or did you?"

"Of course I didn't spray paint it," Doreen cried out. "Why would you even ask that?"

"Just checking," she muttered. "Besides, I wasn't thinking that you would have. I mean, it made no sense for you to do that."

"No, it doesn't make any sense for me to do that," she declared, glaring into the phone. She sighed and pinched the bridge of her nose. "Mack thinks it's got to be somebody I talked to over this current case and figures that I've pissed somebody off. Again."

"Well, you do have a habit of doing that, dear."

Doreen once again glared at her phone. "I seem to be really tired, Nan."

"Oh, of course you are. Never mind me," Nan replied. "I would invite you down for tea, but, if you're really tired, we should probably wait until tomorrow, when you've had a chance to rest."

She nodded. "That would be good, thank you."

"Okay, I'll see you for breakfast then." Without giving Doreen a chance to say anything, Nan rang off.

Doreen frowned. "*Breakfast?* Who said anything about breakfast?"

And was breakfast really what Nan was suggesting? It didn't sound quite right, but then it was Nan. Yet Doreen hated to say it, but she had her concerns about her grandmother's mental health too. And it would break her heart if anything serious was going on. She quickly texted Nan.

What was that about breakfast?

Nan called her back. "You agreed to come for breakfast, dear. Have you forgotten already?"

"You didn't mention breakfast until your parting shot," Doreen added. "So I don't really know what it is that you're planning."

"I'm not planning anything, but, if people are coming after you because you're asking questions, then maybe we need to get some help on this issue. I'll see you what, around seven*ish?*"

"No, not seven," Doreen cried out in horror. "Particularly if I have a bad night."

"Well, goodness," Nan replied, "we certainly don't want to leave it too late, early bird and all that, you know."

Doreen wasn't exactly sure what all that meant in her grandmother's mind, so Doreen aimed for a middle ground, "How about eight?"

"Eight's fine, but don't be late." And with that same singsong cheery voice, she rang off.

Doreen wondered just what kind of *Alice in Wonderland* scenario she kept getting into. She absolutely adored her grandmother, but there were times that she worried her and vexed her too.

But then she was also sure that her grandmother would say the same about Doreen. Still, she was too tired to deal with too much right now. Plus her mind was overwhelmed with emotions about everything that she and Mack had talked about, and what she'd talked about with all the suspects. And yet, it's the first time she really acknowledged that all those people she'd talked to were in theory, suspects. They all had motives; they all had opportunity. Doreen didn't know who was the last person to see Dennis. According to the investigators, that was the wife, as he headed off later in the afternoon to pick up some equipment in town.

The fact that he didn't show up in town meant somebody else had seen him last, or the wife was lying. Doreen thought about everything she'd heard from the wife, but nothing screamed duplicity about Meredith to Doreen. But then, what did she know? It seemed as if people had all kinds of ways of showing off and being other than who they really were. It was kind of distressing in a way.

Tired, a little bit worn out, and edgy, Doreen tidied the house, locking up everything and setting the security. Then she went upstairs, had a hot bath, and went to bed.

Chapter 27

Thursday Morning...

UPON WAKING, DOREEN rolled and stretched, delighted that she had slept a solid night through. She contemplated her day. Cleaning the paint off the deck was obviously on top of her to-do list. However, as she checked her watch, she noted it was already one-quarter to eight. Groaning at that, she dashed out of bed, quickly dressed, and, with the animals in tow, headed down the creek to Nan's. As soon as she got there, she sat down hard at the patio table and announced, "I didn't get coffee."

Nan eyed her and said, "Let's get the tea on then. It's not quite the same caffeine hit, but it should help." And, with that, she bustled into the kitchen.

Goliath, in an unusual mood, curled up on Doreen's lap and just snuggled in. She bent over and hugged him gently, breathing in the wonderful scent of the cat, while he purred against her ears. Thaddeus reached over and pecked Goliath on top of the head, but the cat didn't even move, didn't even open an eye. Doreen scolded Thaddeus.

"He's fine. You have no need to be jealous. Goliath rarely sits in my lap, and you are on my shoulder. So you guys can get along for a few minutes." At that, Thaddeus pecked Goliath again. She tapped the bird lightly on the head. "Stop." Thaddeus did it again and then again. Finally out of patience she tapped him lightly on the beak and muttered, "Stop."

He glared at her and said, "Thaddeus loves Nan."

Nan chose that moment to come out, and she smiled. "And Nan loves you too, Thaddeus." He squawked and tried to get over to her.

"He's just mad at me," Doreen explained, "because I wouldn't let him keep poking at Goliath."

Nan looked at her like she lost her mind. "He never hurts Goliath."

"*Hurt* is one thing," Doreen noted. "Being an irritating younger brother is a whole different story."

Nan burst out in delighted laughter. "Oh my, it is a joy to see them getting along so well."

"I don't think this is getting along so well," Doreen stated, looking at her grandmother. "Lots of times they just fight."

"And lots of times they don't fight," she replied.

"I'll give you that," Doreen muttered. "I don't just know when it'll be one or the other."

"Just like having children, you never really know, until they erupt with their next problem," Nan said, with a smile.

Doreen didn't say a whole lot to that. She hadn't had any children, and looking after the animals was more than enough at this point. "Goliath seems to be unusually cuddly." She leaned over and pet the large cat gently. "He is right now anyway, which is also why Thaddeus was poking at him, I'm sure." She wondered whether Thaddeus could be jealous.

"They do get very jealous," Nan replied. "You can't blame them. Thaddeus generally gets everything he wants."

"I know, almost too much so." Doreen sighed, as Thaddeus squawked at her and cuddled up to Nan. "He's also very much the kind to play one against the other." She pointedly looked at the bird.

Nan shook her head. "You can't give them human qualities. You know that, dear."

"Sure I can," she muttered, but she relented. "I love them all equally. Don't worry, Nan."

"I'm not worried," she said, as she patted Doreen's hand. "I do want to ensure everybody's happy though."

And, of course, that's the bottom line. Nan was just looking out for everybody. When Goliath rolled over and almost fell off her lap, he opened his eyes and glared at her.

She caught him before that happened. "Sorry, Goliath. I guess I was sleeping on my job, wasn't I?" He closed his eyes, fully expecting her to continue holding him. And he was still playing his games when the tea was ready and while Nan was busy pouring it.

When Doreen shifted to get closer to the tea, Goliath opened his eyes and glared at her. "You could get down, you know," she muttered. "You don't have to make me your servant all day long." Goliath slipped to the floor, sauntered over to the big flower bed, hopped up, and curled up in the middle of it, as if he hadn't had a good nap in days. And considering Doreen hadn't had a whole lot of sleep the last few nights, maybe that was his problem too. Mugs, on the other hand, was stretched on his side under her chair, snoring gently.

"Everybody seems tired today," Nan pointed out.

Doreen nodded. "Yeah, the vandalism at the house yesterday kind of upset everybody."

Nan lost her curious look, and obvious worry crept in. "I do worry about you up there," she muttered.

"Don't," Doreen replied. "We're fine. We set the alarm each night. I just think the animals are as worried about their deck as I am."

"So is it the deck you're worried about," Nan asked, with a smile, "or the intruder?"

"Honestly, mostly the deck," she replied. "I'm not even sure how to fix it."

"They really spray-painted all over it?"

Doreen pulled out her phone and showed her grandmother some of the pictures that she'd taken.

"Oh my, that's terrible."

She was just as outraged as Doreen was, which made her feel much better. "It is terrible, and I don't like the fact that somebody seemed to think that that was the way to treat my place. I don't know how to fix it."

"I'm pretty sure you can sand that right down again and restain it," Nan suggested, "although you might need bigger tools than you have."

"I've got lots of tools in the garage that I have yet to use, so maybe that's what I'll do this weekend."

"It would be a good idea, yes, particularly if the sight of this will bother you too much."

"Of course it'll bother me," she declared, looking at Nan. "How could it not?"

Nan shrugged. "I mean, it would upset me, but I didn't want to make too much of it in case you were okay with it."

"Of course I'm not okay with it," Doreen exclaimed, and then closed her eyes. "Sorry, I shouldn't be so short-tempered. This has got me a bit on edge."

"I see that," Nan said. "Maybe you should back off this case."

"No, that's not happening," Doreen declared. "Can't afford to do that."

"Why not?" Nan asked. "Surely nobody would mind if you did. I mean, after all, if you're getting harassed …"

"Maybe they wouldn't mind, but *I* would," Doreen stated. "I don't like the idea of anybody coming after me to do something like this to the extent that I step away from it all. You and I both know how important it is that we get to the bottom of this and any other cold cases."

"Sure, but we also don't want you to get hurt in the process," she pointed out.

"Mack will talk to the captain about it today."

"Oh, good. I'm so glad you have Mack."

"Me too," Doreen agreed, with feeling. "He's been wonderful in all this."

Nan nodded wisely. "I'm glad to hear that, dear."

Doreen looked over at her suspiciously, but nothing in her expression gave away anything, other than a quiet satisfaction.

"What about that ex-husband of yours?"

"Still working on the divorce, getting everything signed by him," she muttered. "Although I'm hoping that process will come to a successful end here real soon."

"With any luck it will, but it might take longer than you're expecting. They usually do."

"I'll call Nick on my way home and see if he has the final paperwork yet."

"Good, do that." Nan smiled and nodded. "Enjoy the tea, and I'll go get breakfast."

She watched as her grandmother went back inside again.

Doreen wasn't sure what her grandmother was up to, but just then the patio door opened, and Richie and Maisie came out, bearing plates. Richie had a big smile on his face.

"See? We really like it when you come to visit," he greeted her in a conspiratorial voice.

"We get all kinds of goodies." Maisie rolled her eyes at her.

She stared at them, noting both held platters of mini quiches, sausage rolls, and God-only-knows what else. She stared at the spread. "Wow. What brought this on?"

Richie said, "I told them that you are working on a new case and that you were coming to discuss it."

"Oh."

He patted her hand and explained, "Don't worry. They know it's for you and that you are here. I wouldn't try to dupe them."

She winced at that. "It would be nice if you wouldn't make it about me though," she replied. "I'm not a resident here. It makes me feel bad to eat your food."

"That's because you're a good person." Richie grinned at her. "Besides, I needed something new to bug them with anyway."

She rolled her eyes at that. "You could just not bug them."

"I could," he agreed, with a bright, cheerful grin, "but then what will I do? They'll think I am sick and call the doctor on me."

At that, Doreen burst out laughing. "Well, that might be. I admit that I probably would too."

He nodded. "See? Everybody expects me to do something," he stated. "So, if I don't do it, then they're all disappointed."

"I don't know about the disappointment part," Doreen muttered, "but it would be nice if we could keep this so it's not just because I'm coming."

He looked over at Nan, who rolled her eyes. "See? I told you. She's a stick in the mud for doing things the right way."

"Well that's not a bad thing," Maisie said, joining in the conversation. "We need people like her."

"Oh, I know," Nan replied in disgust, "but she can be a bit of a party pooper."

Doreen stared at Nan in horror. "You did not just say that to me."

"Did so," she muttered, as she plunked down at the table across from her. "But we have the treats, so let's eat." And, with that, she snagged two mini quiches. Everybody else helped themselves too.

Doreen realized that she was in danger of getting nothing. She quickly snagged two different items. "These look delicious."

"You know they cooked it especially for you, right?" Richie asked.

Oh dear God…

Through brunch or breakfast, she wasn't even sure what you called a meal like this, the conversation was about everything *but* her case.

Finally Richie put the last bite in his mouth, waiting until he'd swallowed it, and then asked, "Now what's this about that beautiful deck of yours getting spray-painted?"

She quickly explained. It was hard to get it all out though because Maisie kept exclaiming at everything Doreen said.

Finally Nan rapped Maisie smartly on the leg. "Stop, dear. Poor Doreen is having enough trouble getting things out without you complicating everything."

Maisie gazed at Nan, hurt in her eyes and then back at Doreen.

Doreen smiled at her. "It's fine. I really don't have anything else to say."

Nan snorted. "Why didn't you say so then? Here we thought you had a big story to tell us."

She shook her head. "No, Nan, no big story."

"Well, that wasn't very much news then. I am not very impressed about that deck though," she muttered.

"No, neither am I. It was a lovely deck, and I'm really sorry that somebody would have done that to it."

"Surely it can be fixed though."

She nodded. "Mack told me that it can. I'm just not sure what the process will look like."

"Right," Richie replied, "because it takes time to repair that damage."

"It does, indeed, but I'm on that deck constantly. So it's quite an eyesore right now and, of course, a bad memory."

Richie nodded in commiseration. "Exactly. You need to fix it for that reason alone. We can't have you looking at it and getting upset every time you see it."

"No, I would hope not," she murmured. She looked over at him. "I do thank you for thinking of me in terms of food."

"Can't have you starving, my dear." Richie puffed up with importance. "You're too important to this community."

Doreen burst out laughing. "I don't know about that. I think somebody in the community would like me to stop what I'm doing."

"There's always somebody who wants you to stop though," Richie stated comfortably. "You just keep doing what you're doing. Do it safely, of course, but keep doing what you're doing."

"Well, that's the plan. I'll have to go soon and rattle a few more cages today."

"Which ones?" Maisie asked, leaning forward excitedly. "Is there anything we can do to help?"

Doreen pondered that and then slowly shook her head. "I don't think so. It involves my talking to everybody again. It would be nice if I knew who owns that big black truck that's been following me too."

At that, Richie slowly lowered his teacup. "Somebody is following you?"

"I think it's two different trucks, one new black one and one old beat-up one. Still, I suspect it's the same person," she suggested. "Otherwise that would be too much to expect that there would be *two* people following me."

"It depends how many people you've upset," Nan said. "How many are there?"

Doreen eyed her grandmother. "I have no idea. … I didn't think anybody would be upset enough to follow me. Yet you know people can always take things in a different way."

"Well, you are rattling their cage," Maisie said, with a chuckle.

Doreen smiled at that. "Absolutely, and I won't exactly give it up right now either."

"Oh, you can't. Absolutely you can't," Maisie replied in horror. "They would have won then."

"I don't know that it's even about winning, as much as it is about ensuring that Dennis is found."

"Dennis is probably dead," Maisie stated. "I mean, there's no reason for him to still be alive. I think the consensus is that he's dead, but nobody has any proof either way. He probably died right away."

Privately Doreen agreed with Maisie, but Doreen didn't have any proof of that. "Even if he did die right away," Doreen replied, "I would still need some proof."

"Such a problem, isn't it?" Nan asked.

"What is?" Doreen asked, as she looked at the platters.

"The onus of finding proof."

Doreen nodded. "Yes, but that's what justice is all about, confirming we don't convict the wrong person."

"And then the right people often get away with it anyway," Maisie complained in disgust. "I mean, you just have to watch all those TV shows to see how many times the bad guys get away with murder."

"Sometimes," Doreen replied, not sure where this conversation was going.

"But a lot of the time the police do really good jobs." Maisie stared at Doreen.

"That's because you're biased," Nan chipped in.

Doreen winced at that. "Maybe, but I also am working on the side of the law," she added, "so I would like to think that we're winning."

At that, Maisie chuckled. "The police are winning because you're on it," she shared, with a note of satisfaction. "If you weren't solving all these cases, they would be sitting there, getting even colder."

"Maybe," Doreen muttered. "but it takes a lot of time to sit there and rattle their cages." She gave an eye roll at the terminology.

"Exactly, and because you are, it's also putting you in danger. So really the police should be giving you protection," Maisie proclaimed.

"Well, I've got Mack," Doreen pointed out, with a note of humor.

"But he doesn't live with you, dear," Nan said. "I would feel so much better if he did."

"He has his own house, and he likes his own space."

"You mean, you like your own space."

She glared at her grandmother and nodded. "Yes, that's true. I do. I haven't had a whole lot of it, and I plan on enjoying it."

At that, Richie patted her hand. "That's fine. You do what you need to do. We'll just be along for the ride to help."

"Along for the ride?" she asked, suspiciously looking from Nan to Richie to Maisie.

Richie nodded, adding, "We'll be here waiting for you, keeping track of all the information, making sure that it doesn't go awry."

She wasn't exactly sure what he was talking about, but they were all nodding agreeably, as if this was a plan they had already made in their heads.

On that note she decided to skedaddle while she still could, so they wouldn't be getting more into her face about it. She scooped up the animals, thanked Richie again for the breakfast, and then started walking home.

Nan called out, "Please do be careful, child."

"Will do, Nan," Doreen replied, with a hand raised. And she disappeared around the corner.

Chapter 28

On Doreen's way home, her animals had decided to fall back into their normal routine, and everybody was eager to enjoy the river. Mugs was dancing in and out of the water, getting more wet than she would have liked.

Thaddeus rode on her shoulder, not too bothered about the water but still keenly watching Goliath, who was definitely walking away from the water, trying to stay out of Mugs's way, especially as he came out and sprayed everything in front of him. She hadn't got more than ten minutes up the pathway, when she heard footsteps coming up behind them. She turned to see a tall, spare man she didn't know. He tipped his hat to her and kept on walking. She realized just how nervous she was becoming.

Calling Mugs to her, she continued on to her property. It was only ten o'clock in the morning, and time to get her head wrapped around her day and to figure out what she would do next. She didn't know and hadn't seen who the driver of either of the black trucks was, and she didn't get a license plate or a make and model. So that was a complete dead end. And she could only blame herself for that. She should have been trickier and come up behind him and got the plate number.

As for the person who'd damaged her deck, well, karma was coming after him. Doreen had to stop and realize that it could easily have been a woman too. Doreen didn't know who had been there and didn't know if anybody else had seen her vandal. The spray painter could have come up the back pathway, gone into her yard, sprayed her deck, and taken off, with nobody being the wiser.

Richard hadn't seen anybody, and that made her stop and look over at her neighbors on the other side—Cindy and Josh. Doreen continued down to the creek, past her house, and walked along Cindy and Josh's fence, but it was a wooden fence all the way around their property. With Doreen's rear fence line taken down months ago, it made for easier access to her backyard from the creek than to get into Richard's backyard or Cindy and Josh's.

Doreen called over the fence, "Hello, hello," but she got no answer. So she headed up through her backyard to the front yard with her animals, and then walked over to the neighbors on her right.

When she knocked on the door, both Cindy and Josh answered, and, as usual, were dressed in matching outfits— khaki pants and pink T-shirts. They both looked harried, one child in her arms and another child in his.

"Hey," Cindy greeted her, relieved when she saw Doreen. "We're on babysitting duty. You okay?"

"I am, I just wondered if you had seen anybody at my place yesterday. Somebody came in and spray-painted my beautiful deck."

Cindy looked at her in astonishment. "Oh my, I don't know anybody who would do that.'

"No, I don't know either," Doreen muttered. "I just

wondered if you'd heard anything."

Cindy and Josh shook their heads in unison, and then one of the children started screaming and fighting to get down. Cindy groaned. "I'm sorry. It's hard for me to hear anything over these guys sometimes."

Doreen nodded. "So you haven't seen anybody skulking around the cul-de-sac or by the creek or anything like that?"

Cindy shook her head. "No, sure haven't. Richard might have."

"I did talk to him already," Doreen replied, "and he didn't see or hear anybody either."

"I'm sorry. We can't do much for you then." With that, Cindy and Josh backed away with the grandkids and shut the door.

Doreen let them escape. After all, if they had nothing to offer, they couldn't help Doreen. As she slowly walked back over to her place, Richard called out to her. She looked over at him, standing on his front porch. "What's up?" she asked.

"Did you find out who it was?"

She shook her head. "No, I didn't. I was just asking Cindy if she'd seen anything."

He snorted. "Have you ever seen her and Josh outside?"

She pondered that and shook her head. "No, I haven't."

"They're always in the house," he stated. "It's really not a good way to raise kids—or grandkids, in their case."

"Maybe not, but I guess we don't really have any right to judge anyone," she replied.

He shook his head at her. "Why not? Everybody judges us."

She didn't really have much of a chance to argue that because, for one, he was right, and, for another, it was a hard argument to have when they didn't really see eye to eye on a lot of issues. "But if nobody saw anything, it doesn't make any bit of a difference anyway," she finished glumly.

"Maybe, but you mentioned that one truck that came along here the other day, driving through the cul-de-sac. And the guy who walked through here the other night."

"I did see the truck come through the cul-de-sac, but I didn't get a full license plate just a couple of letters and that's only because he drove past and the neighbor's garage light flicked on."

He reeled off the letters.

"You saw that?" she asked in astonishment.

"Ever since that deal with Roscoe, I've been keeping a little bit closer eye."

"You're afraid that somebody will come after you because of Roscoe?"

"Not necessarily," he replied. "I just think, once you've been touched by some of this, it makes you a little more wary."

"That it does," she murmured. "Do you remember anything else about the driver?"

"Just a big man. That's all I remember."

"Okay, I'll give the letters to Mack." He nodded and disappeared inside, before she had a chance to even say *thank you*. She walked back to her house and quickly texted Mack what Richard had shared.

He phoned her instead. "He told you that?"

"Yes, but only after I went to the neighbors on the other side of me—Cindy and Josh—and asked them if they had seen anything in my backyard. After the last cold case with Roscoe, his brother, that's when Richard told me how he was paying more attention to the area around him. He didn't recognize the truck or the driver, but he was driving so slowly around our cul-de-sac that I imagined he noted the license plate numbers, just in case."

"That's good," Mack replied, "because that's the kind of help we do need. Too often everybody is just blind to what's going on around them, and things like license plates aren't on their radar."

"I don't know that it'll lead to anything," Doreen muttered, "but it is something."

"Hey, we'll take it," Mack said. "I'll get back to you in a few minutes." With that, he ended the call.

She was still kind of upset and out of sorts as she walked inside. So she decided to do a bit of housekeeping, something that needed to be done, yet she just didn't spend enough time doing it. With that thought, she dedicated herself to sweeping and mopping floors and then went up to her room, stripped the bedding, and put on laundry. With the animals sleeping on the bed all the time, the hair accumulation was something else.

Mugs was never allowed on the bed when she was married, and the housekeeper took care of all that. Now it was just a never-ending flow of dog hair and cat hair. She couldn't just blame poor Mugs for it all, not when Goliath seemed to shed just as much.

By the time she was done with that, she'd worked up a bit of a sweat, so she opened up all the windows in the place to air it out and then remade her bed. Afterward she came back down and put on the coffee that she had missed out on this morning. Even as she did, she heard a truck coming. She raced to the front window, and, sure enough, it was that black truck again.

She watched as he pulled into the cul-de-sac and ever-so-slowly drove up and around. She didn't know whether he was looking to see her specifically, somebody else who might be home alone, or what was going on generally in this neighborhood.

She watched as he got up to the crest close to her place, and then he drove even more slowly. She stepped out onto the front porch and waved at him. He hit the brakes, then churned forward, as if in shock and horror, and raced out of the cul-de-sac. She laughed. "Yes, sucker. I saw you." Of course she hadn't seen a whole lot, just a man whose head was mostly hidden by the visor, and he appeared to be clean shaven. She couldn't tell much more than that.

As she turned back to step into her front door, she saw Richard standing there on his front porch.

"That was him, wasn't it?" he asked.

"I don't know yet. I didn't catch the license plate."

"I caught 3 letters, enough to consider it's the same truck."

"Good. I gave that to Mack earlier. I'll tell him that we just had our visitor back again."

Richard *harrumphed* and headed back inside his house, but this time he seemed to be more on her side than against her.

As she updated Mack, he replied, "The truck belongs to somebody I need to talk to."

"He just left my place, so I don't know where he's going."

"Chances are he's heading home after that scenario. I'll go to his place, have a talk with him, and then come back to your place."

"I just put coffee on, so I should have the whole pot finished before you get here." And, with that, she disconnected. She burst out laughing, feeling good for the first time all day.

And then she set about cleaning up the kitchen, something that she didn't really take enough time to do either. It's not that she was messy or dirty, but cleaning didn't come automatically to her. How odd to think that something like that wasn't a natural trait and was something she had to be trained to do. Maybe if she'd been brought up having to do things, like keeping her own bedroom, she would be accustomed to it, but nope. It seemed like, for her, this was all about breaking the bad habits of her marriage, so that she became somebody who could look after herself.

When she heard another truck whip through the cul-de-sac about twenty minutes later, she raced to the front window once again. It was a black truck, but it was a different black truck. Well, no, she wasn't sure about that. She couldn't see the license plate to confirm that.

Richard also stood outside on his front porch. He shook his head. "It's a different one."

Doreen nodded. "Well then, he's not after me."

Richard snorted. "You could have half the town after you," he muttered. "Everybody has something against you."

"I'm a nice person," she protested.

"Yeah, but you piss people off."

"That's not fair," she muttered. "I'm just trying to help."

He laughed at her. "Well, this is the kind of response you're getting then."

She glared at him and stepped back inside. The truck was long gone, but it didn't sound the same as the other one either. So she was pretty sure it was a different one, as Richard confirmed. Probably somebody just lost.

When Mack pulled up, she didn't even bother racing out to the front yard. Mugs acted as if Mack were here, so she knew who it was. When he came into the living room, she looked at him.

"After the first black truck came today again," she said, "another black truck came afterward. Different license plate, different kind of truck, so I have no idea who it was."

He nodded. "Well, the one truck, the beat-up one, belonged to Rodney, the guy who went to jail for beating up Dennis Polanski."

She stared at him. "Really?"

He nodded. "But he denies having anything to do with your deck, saying he just wanted to stop and ask you if you had any information on the case and didn't know how to approach you. He feared he would be taken the wrong way, so he didn't stop. He is a big guy, so he does appear to be threatening in that respect. Did he do anything threatening?"

She shook her head. "No, I mean, … I wondered if he was the one who followed me that day, but I didn't know for sure if anyone was following me."

"And, even if it was him, that's not exactly a crime." Mack shook his head. "I don't like it. This guy already has a record for assault."

"And we don't need him to get into trouble again," she said, with a nod. "Last thing we want to do is push him back down that path of crime."

He stared at her. "Look. I don't care whether he goes back down that pathway or not, as long as it's not with you."

She beamed at him. "There's your softie heart again."

He sighed. "I'm trying to keep you safe."

"Yeah, I know that. What will it take for you to dig up a body?"

"What do you mean?" he asked. "Or do you mean *exhume* a body? You know we just went through all that mess at the cemetery."

"Yeah, but we knew there wasn't a body in any of those graves of interest."

"No, we didn't know that," he clarified in exasperation. "*You* thought that, but we didn't have proof of that until we opened them."

She sighed. "Okay, what will it take to dig up a body?"

He shook his head. "If we knew for a fact that there *was* a body and that we needed to get DNA or something from it, that's a different story."

She nodded. "Because really this case, at the heart of it, is very simple. I just don't know who ended it."

He sat down in front of her. "What are you talking about?"

"Dennis, the missing person I'm working on."

"Yes, what about him?"

"It's obvious that he's been murdered, and it's obvious where he is," she shared, "but there are too many suspects to sort out who killed him. If we don't lock that down, nobody will pay for the crime."

He looked at her. "Are you serious? You think you already know where Dennis is?" He stared at her in shock.

"I'm pretty sure I know where he is, but I don't know who did it."

He stared at her. "You're thinking of that garden, aren't you?"

She nodded. "I absolutely am."

He nodded. "If we were to bring in a cadaver dog, that would help." He stared at her. "What makes you think his body is there?"

"Well, for one, Mugs," she replied. "For two, the timing. Although they have a lovely reason for completing the garden, I'm pretty certain the reason itself was just an excuse."

"Who do you think did it?"

"I don't know," she muttered. "That's the problem. An awful lot of people are involved."

"I always wondered about the wife," Mack shared.

"I don't think it is her," Doreen replied. "I think, in fact, it may have been *because* of her, but I don't think she's the one who killed Dennis."

"Why not?"

"Because she's too focused on the farm, too focused on raising her sons and taking care of things."

"Do you think the kids are involved?"

"No, I sure don't, thankfully." She beamed at him. "Lots of other people are though."

"Sure, with all the affairs, too many other people," Mack noted, "and we just never had a reason for any of them to kill Dennis—well, no facts to support that."

"I know. The question is whether it was done alone or in conjunction with somebody else."

At that, he stared at her. "Now you'll say there are two killers?"

"No, I'm not saying anything yet. All I can say is that some people are definitely involved, and I'm pretty sure I know where the body is."

"Even finding the body would be huge, but I need more than just, *Hey, Mack. I think the body's there.*"

"I know," she muttered. "That's where the problem lies."

"And you can't go traipsing around on private property," he warned.

She winced at that. "Of course not. That's not allowed either, is it?"

"No, sure isn't."

She nodded. "Fine then, I'll just have to get sneaky." He stared at her in alarm. She shrugged. "It's okay. I know how to be sneaky."

He glared at her. "Getting sneaky often means getting hurt."

"I haven't done anything to deserve getting hurt by anyone," she protested.

"No, but it sure sounds like you're about to."

She smiled. "I could say you can come with me, but then it looks like we set it up."

"Please don't do anything stupid," he said. "We already have this guy following you."

"Do you think he's a danger?" she asked him.

"I don't know what to think about him," Mack admitted. "I mean, he had a plausible reason to seek you out, but is it a good one? I'm not so sure. And I know that, because of his record, it makes me suspicious. His record is also why he didn't want to approach you face-to-face, given his size."

"Because I would be scared of him?"

"Or because you would just naturally be suspicious because of who he is. Once you get a record for assault," Mack pointed out, "that sticks with you for life."

"I guess," she muttered. "And I wouldn't have known about his record, except for the work I'm doing."

"Exactly. And even if a body is in that xeriscape garden, which you keep saying is there, that doesn't give us the right to go in and dig it up to find it, not without some evidence first."

"It would have to be buried deep, so there won't be any smell, won't be anything obvious to us humans. Although trained dogs could tell us, right?"

"But even then, it still won't prove what we need to prove, which is who put the body there, if a body is there. Although it would become an active case then in a big way."

"Exactly," she replied. "And then sometimes I wonder if we should let sleeping dogs lie."

He stared at her. "What do you mean?"

"I'm just wondering … No, don't worry about it. I'll have to think about it."

"Well, you can think about it," Mack said, "but thinking about something like that is a whole different story than trying to sort through the rights and wrongs of a murder."

She nodded. "I know. I know that."

As she headed toward the coffeepot, he asked, "Haven't you had enough coffee already?"

"Nope, sure haven't," she declared. "And every time I stare at my deck out there, I feel like it'll never be enough."

"We can fix it this weekend."

She turned to look at him. "Can we?" she asked hopefully.

"Absolutely. It'll take a bit of sanding, but we can take that off. There's also a slim chance that it's water-based paint," he added, "if it is, you can hose it off. You might want to try that first."

"Oh, I can do that," she cried out in delight, "It never even occurred to me that might be an option."

"Some paints are oil-based, and some are water-based. So it depends what kind was used on your deck. Honestly should have been oil-based, but check."

"Okay, I'll do that soon."

"I can't stay. I've got to run. So please stay inside as much as you can, and stay safe." And, with that, he was gone.

She smiled, headed out to the deck, turned on the hose, and pointed it at the paint. To her delight it did dissolve under the water. "Thank you, thank you, thank you." And with that she spent the next hour scrubbing and washing the deck, until it was back to brand-new again. She beamed, as she stared down at her beautiful deck.

"There you are," she whispered, with a smile. "Now my life feels right again."

Chapter 29

AFTER A RUN for groceries, Doreen walked back into the house, with her shopping in her hand, as she called out to the animals. They weren't at the front door, and then she found the back door wide open. Groaning, she raced out there to find all her animals stretched out, waiting in her backyard. Everything looked completely untouched. She stood and glared.

"Did I really leave without closing this door?" she cried out, and just then Richard poked his head over the fence and almost gave her a heart attack. She was hardly able to suppress a rising scream at his sudden appearance.

"Yeah, you did," he stated. "I poked my head over to see what you were up to, and all the animals were there, and the kitchen door was wide open. Then I heard you driving off along the driveway."

"Oh good Lord. I'm definitely not happy about that."

"Hey, when you get too rattled and you are spread too thin, too focused on some things and not others, it's easy to make those kinds of mistakes."

"Sure, but after somebody has already vandalized my deck, that's hardly something I want to forget."

He looked at the deck and noted, "You got it cleaned."

Such shock filled his tone that she smiled. "Yeah, sure did. I spent a couple hours scrubbing it down."

"Good," he replied. "I didn't think you would ever get that cleaned up again."

"Every once in a while, things work out."

And he gave a *harrumph* and disappeared behind his side of the fence again.

She just smiled, turning to face her animals. "We should probably take care of this other thing, before anybody comes back to warn me off this case." First, she put away the perishable food. With that done, she loaded up the animals and got back into her vehicle—tired, a little bit antsy—and headed toward the Southeast Kelowna farm. When she pulled into the driveway, she hopped out, grabbed the spray paint that she had bought at the grocery store, and started spraying it all over the xeriscape garden.

Several people came running and cried out, "What are you doing? What are you doing?"

She looked up to see Meredith, standing there, glaring at her. And Danny, Johnson, and the son who worked the farm, Joe. She nodded. "Hey, just returning the favor."

"What are you talking about?" Meredith cried out. "Why would you do that?"

"Because your son did that to my property," Doreen declared. "So I figured that there must be some reason why he did it to mine. Therefore, I figured, if I came and did it to yours, we could figure it out together."

Meredith stared at her, like she'd lost her mind. "What are you talking about?"

Doreen pointed at Meredith's son. "Hey, Joe. You want to explain to me why you did this to my deck?" Mugs tugged at his leash, growling in the back of his throat. Thaddeus hid under her hair against her neck. Goliath sat still, except for his tail, which twitched with sharp movements.

Joe glared at her. "Are you crazy?"

"A lot of people would call me crazy. I ignore it because it's not the nicest thing you could say to people."

He just stared at her, shook his head. As he looked at his mom, he stated, "She's nuts. I didn't do anything."

"But you did," Doreen clarified. "You came to my place. You went into my backyard, and you spray-painted my brand-new deck. I'm trying to figure out why. So here I am."

"So you came and vandalized my property to get answers?" Meredith asked, looking at her in shock.

"That's what your son did to mine."

Meredith frowned, shaking her head. "Nobody does that. Who does that?"

Doreen shrugged. "Seemed like a good idea at the time."

"You're nuts," Joe snapped.

Doreen glared at him. "You're the one who came and vandalized my place." He just continued to glare at her, but she caught the shift of his gaze away from her. And she knew she was right. "Why?" she asked. "I'm not going away until you tell me why."

"Or I could call the cops," Meredith declared, with a snort. "That will take care of you fast enough."

"Sure it will, and then we'll do some digging into the xeriscape garden," Doreen replied. "How do you feel about that?"

Meredith glared at her in shock. "What are you getting on about?"

Doreen gazed at the son, at Joe's great-grandfather Johnson, and then at Joe's grandfather Danny. "We've got a lot of generations here, all involved in Dennis's disappearance one way or another," Doreen muttered. "So maybe one of you should speak up."

"No," said Johnson, the great-grandfather. "Believe me now, Danny Boy? Like I said, she's nothing but trouble."

Meredith's father, Danny, frowned in bewilderment. "I don't understand what's going on."

"Neither do I." Meredith glared at Doreen. "You know you're crazy, right?"

"I would appreciate it if you would stop saying that," Doreen replied. "Your husband didn't run away. He died. And not only did Dennis die, but he died right here. And you guys buried him in that garden."

"You're crazy," Meredith cried out. "We put this garden in for everybody to honor him, not to bury him."

"*You* may not have known about it, but your grandfather Johnson sure did. So did your son Joe." At that, Doreen turned to face Joe. "Right, Joe?"

Joe stared at her, and his bottom jaw worked ever-so-slightly.

"Go ahead, Mugs. Show me where it is." She unclipped his leash.

At that, Mugs raced forward into the middle of the xeriscape, and—right at the center of the *X* she'd painted—he lifted a leg and peed all over it.

"That's a pretty good marker there," she muttered, with a laugh, only no one else joined in her brand of humor. There was only shock, as everyone stared at her dog, as Mugs ran back over to Doreen. "So, shall we bring in a cadaver dog, or will you spare us the cost of that and just confess?"

"There won't be any confession," Meredith's father, Danny, roared in outrage. "How dare you accuse us of that?"

And right beside him, his father Johnson muttered, "Told you that she would be trouble."

Doreen faced Johnson and grinned. "You've been expecting that kind of trouble ever since you killed Dennis, haven't you, Johnson?"

He just stared at her steadily.

"Right, you didn't kill him. Your great-grandson did. He heard the fight going on between his father and his mom, realized how bad it was, and, in a fit of temper, attacked Dennis and killed him." She turned to Joe. "Even when you were younger, you were always big for your age, and you came up behind him and smacked him hard, with what? A shovel or something?"

Joe stared at her, shaking his head, but his shoulders slumped, and a rawness filled his tone as he muttered, "A two-by-four actually. I just hit him with a two-by-four."

At that, Meredith spun and looked at him in horror. "What?"

"Yeah, that's what this is all about," Doreen stated. "Lies, lies, and more lies. Coverups, then more deceptions," she added, "and your great-grandfather Johnson helped you, didn't he, Joe?"

Joe nodded slowly and looked over at his great-granddad, but she could see the relief warring with grief and even guilt, as he stared at the old man.

"Johnson and I buried him with the machinery, and then just left him because we didn't really know what to do. Then, when granddad Danny suggested we build a memorial to Dennis, it seemed way too good an idea, and it was a great answer in terms of ensuring he was never dug up again," Joe admitted.

Doreen nodded. "And so Dennis is there, isn't he?"

Joe sighed. "He's right where the dog peed," he whispered. "It's why I've had nightmares for the rest of my life, but you're wrong about why."

"Am I?" she asked, looking at him.

He nodded. "Yes, he came out of the house, after he and Mom had that … fight, a fight that had to do with his affairs, affairs that I didn't even really understand, except that he wanted out of the marriage. He wanted half the farm, and he wanted my brother, not me, but my brother. I confronted him outside, and he launched himself at me." Joe shook his head. "He started hitting on me hard," he muttered. "I didn't have any choice. I was defending myself, and I picked up a two-by-four and just whaled on him."

His eyes welled up with tears, as he looked at his mother beseechingly, as if for understanding, for acceptance. "Something snapped inside me, and I just couldn't handle what he was saying, the thought of ripping apart the family, and his taking my brother and leaving all of us." He shook his head. "I didn't even think. I just picked up a two-by-four, and I started hitting him."

Doreen nodded. "And unfortunately that's all too often how it happens. The good news is, you were defending yourself."

"What's good about it?" he asked, looking at the others with anguish. "*I killed my father.*"

Chapter 30

P^{ING.}

Doreen ducked to the ground, the animals racing towards her. Hearing the shrieks all around, she turned, still crouched down, to see great-granddad Johnson standing there, a shotgun in his hand, glaring at her.

"Like I said, *trouble*," Johnson roared.

Another shot came, and it hit too close to her.

"You need to get out of here, you nosy little witch," Johnson cried out. "My great-grandson did nothing but what he had to do."

At that, Meredith moved forward. "Granddad, put that down."

"No," Johnson snapped. "I won't. That troublemaker will just put Joe in prison. This should never have happened. This is as much your fault as it is Joe's."

Meredith stared at her grandfather in shock. She turned to look helplessly at her father, who was already trying to ease the shotgun from his father's hands. But it was a tussle that wouldn't have a happy ending.

Doreen walked closer. "Look. Regardless of how it happened, you can't just leave Dennis lying here, as an unsolved cold case. Look at all the trauma this has caused for everyone."

"Why not?" Johnson sneered. "That's all he was. He was nothing but a cold case. And he couldn't leave anybody else's bed too cold either," he raged like a volcano. "The guy was a loser. She should never have married him."

"So? Is she to blame for making a poor choice?" Doreen asked him.

"Yeah," Johnson bellowed, "and you? You're nothing but trouble."

"Look who's talking," Doreen replied, standing firm.

"My great-grandsons are good and decent," Johnson stated. "Joe doesn't need to suffer for you."

"Then maybe this should have been handled in a different way. So he wouldn't have nightmares all his life."

"Yeah, you should have just let the sleeping dogs lie," Johnson said.

At that, Joe stepped forward. "Granddad, it needed to come out," he replied, his voice shaky. "I haven't slept in years." At that, his mom stepped forward, reached out a hand. He looked at her and then wrapped his arms around her, and Doreen could see Joe's shoulders shaking, as he cried. "It's all right, Mom. It's all right. It had to be done."

Meredith glared at Doreen. "You really do know how to cause havoc, don't you?"

Doreen shrugged. "Sometimes the truth is like that. I personally believe that we're better off finding out the truth, so that we can all make peace with it and move on," she shared. "At the moment, however, we have a problem with Johnson."

Joe turned to his great-grandfather. "Please put that down. Haven't there been enough people hurt?"

"No, not enough," Johnson argued. "There's room here for one more." He pointed the shotgun at Doreen. "*Her.* I said she was trouble," Johnson turned and looked at Danny, moving the shotgun in his direction. Danny put up his hands. "Dad, come on. Calm down now. Calm down. We don't want anyone else to get hurt. Particularly when there's at least one person who suffered who shouldn't have."

Doreen gave a pointed look at the old man. "Right, Johnson? Think of Joe." But as hard as she looked, she still couldn't see any give in the old man. Then all of a sudden Johnson's shoulders slumped, and he shook his head. "No, maybe not. Maybe it's time after all." He looked at his son Danny, his granddaughter Meredith, and his great-grandson Joe, then a gush of words poured out. "The thing is, that boy didn't kill Dennis. I did."

Inside, Doreen crowed. Finally they were getting at the truth.

Joe, teary-eyed, shook his head. "Nice try, Great-Granddad, but you and I both know I did it."

At that, the great-grandfather sighed. "No, you didn't, son," Johnson said. "When I sent you to keep your mom distracted, I took a shovel to Dennis and finished the job. You hit him all right, but you didn't kill him."

At that, Joe stared at him in shock. "What?"

Johnson nodded. "I let you think that you killed him all these years, and it was really me."

Joe stared in shock. "I didn't kill him?" His voice climbed until it broke, as he stared at his great-granddad in shock, mixed with relief and overlaid with hope.

At that, Doreen was delighted that her suspicions were correct. "See? And that's why things like these need to come to the surface," she cried out in joy. "Joe's been racked with guilt, and Meredith has been unable to move on in her life and, meanwhile, the real culprit is holding a shotgun on the rest of us right now." Doreen glared at the old man. "You can hardly even stand up straight, Johnson," she pointed out, "and still you're threatening everybody."

The old man muttered, "That's enough out of you. I might be getting old, but I'm not so weak that I can't see trouble when I see it coming."

She shook her head as she studied him, watching Mugs circle up behind the old geezer. "You've been protecting that secret for a very long time, and you made your great-grandson suffer for it. Isn't enough *enough*?"

Johnson raised the shotgun and declared, "Not quite."

Just as he went to fire, Mugs jumped the old man, hitting him at the back of his knee. Johnson stumbled, and the gun went off, the shot spitting into the ground harmlessly. Johnson fell too. His son Danny raced over and ripped the shotgun from his hands.

"I can't believe you just did that," he cried out, staring at his father in horror. "And I can't believe that you killed Dennis. Or that you made poor Joe believe he did it all these years."

"Why not?" Johnson asked. "Dennis was useless, didn't know the value of a good day's work, and he sure as heck wasn't any good help around here. You know as well as I do that he was just going to leave and rip apart the place."

"I wanted him to leave too," Danny yelled, "but we don't kill people just to get them to go."

"Yeah, you would give him a payout so he disappeared." Johnson glared at his son. "That's how weak you are. I worked hard for this place," he muttered, staring at Danny still. "I wouldn't let Dennis just run away with it."

"He wasn't running away with any of it," his son roared. "I wouldn't give him much, just enough cash for him to disappear and to leave us alone." He turned and looked at his grandson Joe. "And you," he said, "you should have come to me."

His grandson nodded. "I should have. I should have told Mom too, but Great-Granddad told me not to tell anyone." Joe turned and looked at him. "I can't believe you killed Dad and then let me think I did."

Johnson shrugged. "You were young. You had a whole life ahead of you. I figured you would forget or would find a way to deal with it and would move on with your life. Which you did. Besides, it made it easier to keep you in line."

Joe just stared at him in shock.

Doreen nodded. "Yeah, that's the kind of man you are, all right. Shame on you for letting your grandson believe he killed his own father, and now look at you, Johnson. You're still alive and cranky and making everybody's lives miserable." Doreen knew she should butt out, but Johnson was really pissing her off for what he'd done to Joe and Meredith.

"And you, you're nothing but trouble," Johnson roared.

"Yeah, and you're starting to sound like a broken record," she muttered. She looked over at Meredith. "Now do you understand why the truth has to come out?"

Meredith stared at Doreen in shock, then gazed at her son Joe, even now still traumatized and shaken and pale, and Meredith wrapped her arms around him. "Good Lord, I thought you were having such a hard time dealing with the loss of your father."

He held her close. "I couldn't tell you. Great-Granddad told me that I couldn't tell anybody. And now I find out it's because he killed Dad," He turned to face Doreen. "I know you might not believe this right now, but I really do appreciate this."

She nodded. "Good. In this case, you're one of the victims. And I'm really glad to hear that. I wasn't sure who I would see rotting in jail at the end of the day in this case."

Meredith asked Doreen hesitantly, "Do you think Joe will get charged?"

Doreen shook her head. "No, I don't, but I do know we need to get the police in here. And we need to bring in somebody to take your husband out of this grave."

Meredith stared at Doreen and recoiled. "The number of times I stood here, hating him, because of what he'd done, taking off on us like he did," she shared, "and to realize that he was here the whole time?" She shook her head, looked over at her father, tears coming to her eyes. "Good God, what have we become?"

Her father raced over, wrapped up both of them in a hug, and said, "We're just people. We're just people."

On the ground behind everybody, with Mugs at his feet and with the shotgun well away from him, Joe's great-grandfather started to laugh. "Lord, you can't even do anything to me. I'm so old I won't even make it to trial." He started to cough just then, and the son walked over to his dad and helped him to stand up straight.

"That may be," Danny agreed, "but you'll have to take what you've done to the grave with you and hope for forgiveness there."

The old man shrugged. "Couldn't care less about that. Dennis got what he deserved."

Not that Doreen agreed or disagreed, but, wow, things really had come to a head. She let out a slow, deep breath, and Thaddeus poked his head out from behind her hair and cried out, "Is it safe? Is it safe?"

She laughed. "It's safe. You're fine."

"Thaddeus is fine. Thaddeus is fine." And he fluttered his wings out in a full-body shake.

Meredith frowned at the bird on her shoulder and shook her head. "You're definitely memorable."

"Maybe," Doreen said, as she pulled out her phone. "Thankfully this time nobody else got hurt."

Meredith nodded, with tears in her eyes. "For that I'm grateful." She stared over at her granddad Johnson. "I still can't believe it." And then she looked at her son, and the tears came to her eyes again. "What you went through …"

"I know. Even now I can't believe what I'm hearing." Joe stared at his great-grandfather, fury in his eyes.

Doreen, her phone in one hand, calling Mack, reached out with the other hand to Joe and added, "Remember. A lot of people suffered over this. Don't make it any worse than it is."

Joe glanced at her and squeezed her hand, adding a deep sigh. "I get it."

"You've got a whole new life coming," she reminded him, "one that's free of guilt. So make the correct choices right now and let this one go. I know it's hard. I know that you've suffered more than you should have, but you are capable of walking past it. And you have a special reason to do so."

Meredith shook her head. "What's she talking about?"

He snatched his mom up into his arms. "Lisa is pregnant. You'll be a grandma."

Meredith seemed to be in shock. Looking at her father, back at her son, and now at Doreen, Meredith cried out in joy and hugged her son tightly. "Oh my." Meredith turned to Doreen and asked, "You knew?"

"When I talked to your son up at the grocery store yesterday"—she shook her head—"can't believe it was just yesterday, but that's when he told me."

Joe nodded. "She was asking all kinds of questions, and we were talking about a future in life, and I just realized how much all of this was still impacting me," he muttered. "I wanted to say something to you, Mom, but I didn't know how."

"Of course you didn't know how," Meredith agreed sadly. "I'm so sorry you went through this."

They all still stood outside, talking, when Mack drove up in a black-and-white. He and Chester hopped out. Mack took one look at Doreen and frowned.

Chester asked, "What? No dead bodies? No injured people?"

Mack asked, "What's going on, Doreen? Are you losing your touch?"

She grinned at Mack. "Oh, I don't think so. We solved the mystery of the missing husband and father, and we found out that he didn't just walk away. Dennis was murdered. Compliments of Great-Granddad Johnson over there." Doreen pointed to where the old man was glaring at them all.

"What?" Chester's jaw dropped. "Seriously?" He walked over to the old man and asked, "Johnson, did you really do that?"

He snorted. "Somebody had to have the balls to do it," he declared. "That man was a menace." And, at that, he shut up.

Mack scratched his forehead. "I'll need a whole lot more

of a statement than that," he muttered.

Doreen turned to Joe. "I think Joe needs to tell you that story," she suggested, "but it might take a while."

In actual fact, it didn't take very long at all. By the time Joe finished talking, his great-granddad confirmed it all.

Mack stood in shock, as he eyed the xeriscape. "Dennis is really in here, *huh?*"

"He's really in there," Doreen confirmed. "I told you so."

He nodded. "I don't know about the rest of you, but Doreen's got this knack for finding this kind of stuff. She ran across this drone image taken one day of your property, and she latched on to this spot. I told her about your missing person's case, and that was it. She was off to the races."

Joe stared at her. "Did you really just see that xeriscape from a drone and see my dad there?" he asked in confusion.

"Not so much that he was there but that the garden was definitely built with an *X* design—the same *X* that I more or less just made with the red spray paint," she explained. "The way the garden was divided in quadrants, as seen from the sky, it really looked like *X* marked the spot," she noted, with a smile. "And, of course, it was a fanciful notion, but one I couldn't let go of. Matter of fact, as it turned out, I was right."

Joe nodded. "We never thought of it that way, you know?"

"Good," she said. "And remember. You're not going to think of it that way at all anymore. Your dad will be reburied, as he should be, and you will get the closure that you need to move on."

He gave her a boyish smile. "Thank you, thank you so much."

And, with that, Meredith walked over and gave Doreen a hug. "I had no idea," she muttered. "Believe me. At times I absolutely hated this xeriscape garden," she declared, as she stared at it. "It just seemed as dry and as lifeless as my marriage had been. I was so conflicted over it all. That Dennis could walk away and leave us like he had was just the worst scenario I could imagine." Meredith sighed. "Yet the worst part was really about having no answers, never any answers." Meredith turned and glared at her grandfather Johnson. "And all the time the answers were right there."

Her grandfather just stared at her, still the patriarch of the family, generations deep.

Mack walked over, put an arm around Doreen's shoulder, and said, "Nice job."

"In some ways, yes. This closure should help some of them. The others? I don't know. It is a shock regardless."

Mack nodded. "The secrets we try to keep buried."

"They stay buried for only so long," Doreen noted. "That's the problem with secrets. All too quickly somebody sheds light on them, and all the secrets are no more." She let out a big yawn, then groaned. "I'm glad to have this one over with." Doreen looked back at Meredith. "You okay?"

Meredith smiled. "I'm better than I thought I would be. Something is so very freeing about having answers. Even ugly ones."

Doreen smiled at her. "Good. Don't be a stranger next time you're in town. Stop by for coffee."

Meredith looked at her with pleasure and nodded. "Thank you."

Doreen yawned again, and Mack chuckled. "Time for you to go home. We'll be here a while still."

She nodded. "I don't want to necessarily stay, witnessing

when Dennis gets brought to the surface. Personally, I feel that I've done my job." She yawned again and shook her head. "I'll make my way home," she muttered, "and hopefully I can forget about this."

Mack noted the paint and asked her, "Did you do the painting?"

"Oh, yeah," she admitted, "and you can thank Joe for my deck."

He turned and glared at the young man.

Joe flushed. "I know. It was a childish impulse. At the same time I wanted her to stop digging. I have a child on the way, and I was finally able to move on, and here she was digging it all up." He sighed happily. "Thankfully."

At that, she looked over at him. "Well, you're an adult now, so maybe you could try your words and not spray-painting." She motioned at the rocks. "You'll have fun cleaning off all the paint."

"Well, if you used water-based paint, like I did," Joe noted, "it should just hose off. Besides, by the time the tractor and everybody is done in here, digging up stuff, plus a few days of rain, it will be all gone or buried."

She nodded. "That's what I was counting on." And, with that, she headed over to her car, calling the animals to her.

Thaddeus looked back and cried out, "X."

She stopped and frowned. "What did you say?"

He repeated, "X."

"X, yes," Doreen agreed. "X marks the spot." And then she started to laugh.

Thaddeus laughed beside her. "*He, he, he, he. X marks the spot.*" And then he started crowing in this weird bird-like call.

She shook her head. "Okay, I really need to get him home. He's obviously had enough too." And, with a wave at everybody, she got in her vehicle.

Mack waited for her to back up the car, and, as she went to drive forward, he walked over and asked, "Are you okay to drive?"

She smiled. "I'm tired, but I'm okay."

"Good enough. You did good today, and you didn't even get hurt."

"Nope, I didn't." She smiled. "I'm getting better."

"This one wasn't all that easy," Mack noted. "I can see how you were working it, but what if you'd been wrong?" He turned to look at her. "One of these days you'll be wrong, you know?"

"Maybe, but thankfully that day isn't today. I have no idea what's coming next though."

"Forget about what's next," Mack said. "I'll pop by tomorrow, when I get the chance. Go home, rest, and call it a day."

And that's what she did.

Epilogue

Friday Morning…

AFTER A LOVELY night's sleep and a lazy morning inside, Doreen decided to treat herself to Chinese food. Mack was due to come by for lunch, and she thought maybe she could pick up enough for both of them. She had a little bit more money at the moment, and, besides, after the last case closed, she deserved it.

She was pretty sure food therapy wasn't a good thing to get used to, but it was awfully tempting to just keep turning to food every time something good was going on. As she walked down to the Chinese food restaurant that she loved so much, animals in tow, she stepped inside and looked at the menu, just as Mr. Woo came out from the back and asked, "One dish?"

She smiled at him. "Hey, I was hoping to get a couple dishes."

"You always get one dish."

"I'll have company this time," she replied.

"Ah, two dishes."

She winced. "Maybe three."

He looked at her. "Big spender." But his face was splitting into a big smile.

"Not really." Finally settling on three dishes that would hopefully fill her and Mack, she placed her order and paid for it, carefully counting out the money. With lots of money coming, she wondered if she would ever get used to spending it.

"You wait fifteen minutes." Then he shooed her out the door.

She went outside and sat down on a bench. All kinds of noises came all around the place. A normal city day. She sniffed the air and smiled.

She knew Mack had plenty of work to do at Meredith's place, but they had unearthed Dennis yesterday, much to everybody's relief. So, of course, Kelowna was just abuzz with all the news. Doreen didn't really want to get caught up in too much of it, but only so much she could avoid too.

She'd talked for hours with Nan on the phone but had resisted going down to Rosemoor, pleading tiredness. Even now, as she sat here with the animals all around her, she was feeling pretty whomped. But it was a good tiredness.

Goliath wandered over to a shrub and disappeared behind it. She stood up and walked over. "Goliath, come back," she ordered. His head poked through the bush, looked at her, and then he disappeared into a huge cluster of yarrow plants. She smiled at the multicolored flowers.

"Look at the size of those blooms. I've heard you can make tea out of that stuff." She wondered whether that was an old wives' tale or something she could trust. She'd come a long way, but she still had a way to go in terms of knowing what she could do and couldn't do with plants. Google helped, but it also confused her more often than not.

When Goliath started to hiss and snarl, Doreen raced

into the shrubbery, looking for him. "Come out of there," she called to him. She found other flowers, dandelions, and one azalea bush, but this cluster of yarrow seemed to go on and on along the back into another corner. She kept following it. "Goliath? Goliath, come here."

Thaddeus poked his head out from behind her curtain of hair. "Goliath," he called out. "Goliath. Goliath come here."

She glared at him. "You could have told me that you could call him earlier," she muttered.

"*He, he, he, he, he,*" he snickered at her side.

She just sighed. What was she supposed to do when Thaddeus was so completely wise and yet such a little snot sometimes?

"Goliath!" Another howl came, and that was followed by a different animal sound, and all of a sudden the air was filled with cat cries. Doreen raced in that direction, and then out came a spindly-looking cat, who glared at her and sauntered off. Goliath finally came out, strode toward her, his tail up and all puffed out, as if he'd had quite a time. Yet he was strutting, as if he had won the spoils of the war. Something was in his mouth.

Doreen groaned. "What did you find?" she scolded. "Who did you steal it from?"

Of course the other cat was gone, and there was no further sign of him.

Goliath didn't need to steal food from anybody, as he had plenty of food at home. But, as he approached her, he stood up on his back legs and put his front paws on her thighs, and she saw something plastic in his mouth. She snatched it from his mouth. He didn't want to let it go right away, but eventually he released it.

She looked at it and gasped. "Where did you get this?"

she cried out in horror. She raced around to the back of the garden and stopped. She pulled out her phone, and her voice was shaking.

"What's the matter, Doreen?" Mack teased. "I told you that I'll be there in a little bit."

"No, no," she cried out. "You need to come now."

"Doreen, what's the matter?" he snapped. "Are you okay?"

She took a deep breath. "I'm okay, at least for the moment, but I'm not going to be okay for long."

"Stop making cryptic comments and tell me what's going on."

"You need to come to Mr. Woo's Chinese restaurant. I was buying lunch for you and me, and I was waiting on it to walk back home because you were supposed to be there."

"Yes, I'm in the vehicle heading your way. What's the matter?"

"Meet me here now, please." And, with that, she ended the call.

It seemed like an hour, but it was probably not even five minutes before Mack whipped into the parking lot.

He saw her, hopped out, and came running over. "What's the matter?" he cried out.

She stepped back a bit and pointed, and then she held out the plastic item in her hand. "Goliath brought me this, so I went and took a look."

He looked at what was in her hand, frowned, and stepped around the corner. He came back, his face grim. "This is all Goliath brought you?"

She nodded slowly. "Isn't that enough?" she asked. "That's Mathew's driving license," she cried out. "And that's Mathew in that garden bed, isn't it?"

Mack nodded ever-so-slowly, his gaze intense and searching. "I'm sorry, Doreen."

"Sorry won't quite cut it right now," she declared, staring at him. "Somebody killed Mathew."

"Yes. Do you realize what this means?"

She nodded. "Oh, I know what it means. I'm suspect number one."

This concludes Book 24 of Lovely Lethal Gardens: X'd in the Xeriscape.

Read about Yowls in the Yarrow: Lovely Lethal Gardens, Book 25

Lovely Lethal Gardens: Yowls in the Yarrow (Book #25)

Riches to rags. … Marriage is wonderful. … Divorce can be ugly. … Chaos surrounds both …

Doreen has had enough of her estranged husband's antics, but, when he shows up dead in the garden outside her favorite Chinese food restaurant, she's horrified and anxious. And, of course, in the eyes of the rest of the world, … guilty.

There's no Doreen for her to call to help out this time, … but she knows Mack has her back, although he's being questioned too. The police force rallies around her, as their history rips apart her former life and finds out that all her suspicions about Mathew were correct, and he'd been in deep trouble.

The trick now is to make sure that said trouble died with him and won't carry over to Doreen. Good luck with that. Between her animals, the police, and every other well-meaning resident trying to help, Doreen knows she could be in bigger trouble than ever …

Find Book 25 here!

To find out more visit Dale Mayer's website.

https://geni.us/DMSYowls

Author's Note

Thank you for reading X'd in the Xeriscape: Lovely Lethal Gardens, Book 24! If you enjoyed the book, please take a moment and leave a short review.

Dear reader,

I love to hear from readers, and you can contact me at my website: www.dalemayer.com or at my Facebook author page. To be informed of new releases and special offers, sign up for my newsletter or follow me on BookBub. And if you are interested in joining Dale Mayer's Reader Group, here is the Facebook sign up page.
http://geni.us/DaleMayerFBGroup

Cheers,
Dale Mayer

About the Author

Dale Mayer is a *USA Today* best-selling author, best known for her SEALs military romances, her Psychic Visions series, and her Lovely Lethal Garden cozy series. Her contemporary romances are raw and full of passion and emotion (Broken But ... Mending, Hathaway House series). Her thrillers will keep you guessing (Kate Morgan, By Death series), and her romantic comedies will keep you giggling (*It's a Dog's Life*, a stand-alone novella; and the Broken Protocols series, starring Charming Marvin, the cat).

Dale honors the stories that come to her—and some of them are crazy, break all the rules and cross multiple genres!

To go with her fiction, she also writes nonfiction in many different fields, with books available on résumé writing, companion gardening, and the US mortgage system. All her books are available in print and ebook format.

Connect with Dale Mayer Online

Dale's Website – www.dalemayer.com
Twitter – @DaleMayer
Facebook Page – geni.us/DaleMayerFBFanPage
Facebook Group – geni.us/DaleMayerFBGroup
BookBub – geni.us/DaleMayerBookbub
Instagram – geni.us/DaleMayerInstagram
Goodreads – geni.us/DaleMayerGoodreads
Newsletter – geni.us/DaleNews

Printed in Great Britain
by Amazon